"These people don't believe in being subtle..."

The van spun around, performing a one-hundred-and-eighty-degree turn until it faced the little sedan Mustang and Emily were in.

Emily leaned back in her seat and braced herself. "He's going to hit us—"

The van plowed into them, clipping the front driver's-side bumper, sending them spinning toward the curb and a solid light pole.

At the last moment, Mustang swung the steering wheel around. The little car crashed into an old warehouse building, the walls crumbling around them.

"Get out," Mustang said beside her. "Get out now!"

"What about Jay?" she said, looking back.

A shot rang out, echoing inside the building.

"The team will help him." Mustang grabbed her hand and took off running through the dark building.

Emily had no other choice but to follow. She ran, trying her best to keep up with Mustang's longer stride, dodging abandoned crates and pallets.

The sound of several pairs of footsteps pounding behind her kept her moving forward...praying they might have a chance to escape.

FULL FORCE

New York Times Bestselling Author

ELLE JAMES

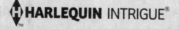

HARLEQUIN INTRIGUE®

Thank you to my wonderful family, who understand when I'm on deadline and allow me the time during holidays to write. Thank you to my mother and father, who taught me the value of hard work and perseverance, without which I would never have finished one book, much less one hundred and fifty! Thank you to my sister, who helps me with brainstorming when I'm fresh out of ideas. Thank you to my editors, who keep me in commas, and commas in the right places! And thank you to our men and women in uniform who protect our country and allow us the freedom to follow our dreams.

Recycling programs
for this product may
not exist in your area.

ISBN-13: 978-1-335-64106-9

Full Force

Copyright © 2019 by Mary Jernigan

Printed in U.S.A.

www.Harlequin.com

Elle James, a *New York Times* bestselling author, started writing when her sister challenged her to write a romance novel. She has managed a full-time job and raised three wonderful children, and she and her husband even tried ranching exotic birds (ostriches, emus and rheas). Ask her, and she'll tell you what it's like to go toe-to-toe with an angry 350-pound bird! Elle loves to hear from fans at ellejames@earthlink.net or ellejames.com.

Books by Elle James

Harlequin Intrigue

Declan's Defenders

Marine Force Recon
Show of Force
Full Force

Mission: Six

One Intrepid SEAL
Two Dauntless Hearts
Three Courageous Words
Four Relentless Days
Five Ways to Surrender
Six Minutes to Midnight

Ballistic Cowboys

Hot Combat
Hot Target
Hot Zone
Hot Velocity

SEAL of My Own

Navy SEAL Survival
Navy SEAL Captive
Navy SEAL to Die For
Navy SEAL Six Pack

Visit the Author Profile page at Harlequin.com.

CAST OF CHARACTERS

Frank "Mustang" Ford—Former Force Recon marine, point man. First into dangerous situations, making him the eyes and ears of the team.

Emily Chastain—Professor of Russian language and part-time interpreter to the Russian embassy.

Nikolai Kozlov—Russian ambassador to the United States, residing at the embassy in Washington, DC.

Sachi Kozlov—The Russian ambassador's wayward daughter.

Viktor Sokolov—The Russian ambassador's trusted assistant.

Tyler Blunt—Investigative reporter.

Jay Phillips—Private investigator hired to follow Tyler Blunt and Sachi Kozlov.

Mack Balkman—Former Force Recon marine, assistant team leader and Declan's right-hand man. Grew up on a farm and knows hard work won't kill you—guns will.

Declan O'Neill—Highly trained Force Recon marine who made a decision that cost him his career in the marine corps. Dishonorably discharged from the military, he's forging his own path with the help of a wealthy benefactor.

Charlotte "Charlie" Halverson—Rich widow of a highly prominent billionaire philanthropist. Leading the fight for right by funding Declan's Defenders.

Augustus "Gus" Walsh—Former Force Recon marine radio operator; good with weapons, electronics and technical equipment.

Cole McCastlain—Former Force Recon marine assistant radio operator. Good with computers.

Jack Snow—Former Force Recon marine slack man, youngest on the team, takes all the heavy stuff. Not afraid of hard physical work.

Chapter One

The Russian ambassador, Nikolai Kozlov, stormed out of the room, his face a mottled red, his black eyes blazing.

Perched on the edge of her seat, Emily Chastain looped the strap of her purse over her shoulder and glanced across the conference table at Viktor Sokolov, the Russian ambassador's executive assistant. She reminded herself that she'd only been the interpreter. The ambassador wasn't mad at her but at the information she'd translated.

Jay Phillips, the private investigator, shoved his notes into a folder and started to slip them into the briefcase he'd carried into the conference room at the Russian embassy.

Sokolov held up his hand. "*Nyet*," he said in a commanding voice. In Russian he continued. "You will leave your papers and data with me."

Emily translated. "He wants you to leave the documents."

Phillips shrugged and laid the folder on the table. "The papers aren't going to change anything. I signed a nondisclosure, and it pays for me to keep what I know to myself. I don't share the information I compile with anyone other than my client. Otherwise, I would have no business."

Emily gave Sokolov a shorter version of what Phillips had said.

Nevertheless the assistant's heavy black brows veed over his nose and he gathered the stack of papers and photographs into a pile in front of him.

Phillips closed his briefcase and pushed to his feet. "Now that the meeting is over, I have an appointment across town in less than an hour."

"If you no longer require my services, I should be going, too," Emily said in Russian.

Sokolov's intense stare turned on Emily. "You will keep the information you have translated private?"

Emily nodded. "I am very discreet. And I signed a nondisclosure agreement when I took this assignment. If we are done here," she said, "I need to use the ladies' room and then I need to leave before the traffic gets too hard to make it back to my apartment before rush-hour traffic gets bad." She spoke the words in Russian.

She started to pick up the notebook in front of her.

A hand came down on the notebook and the ambassador's assistant said, "The notes stay." He, too, spoke in Russian. The hard look on his face brooked no argument.

Phillips stiffened, his eyes widened, but he didn't move from his position by the table.

Her heart beating fast, Emily secured her purse strap on her shoulder and stood. Still shaking from the force of anger the ambassador had displayed, Emily's knees wobbled as she was escorted to the door, alone, without the investigator.

The Russian ambassador had stormed out of the room yelling so loud and fast, Emily couldn't keep up with his Russian. In his wake, the remaining occupants of the small conference room had sat in stunned silence for moments afterward.

Emily couldn't shake a bad feeling about this particular translation gig. The urge to exit the Russian embassy overwhelmed her. As she crossed the threshold of the room she made a quick glance over her shoulder at the investigator. He attempted to leave but the guard behind him pressed a hand to his shoulder and forced him to sit. The American investigator shot a worried glance at Emily. Again, in Russian, she said, "Perhaps Mr. Phillips would like to share a cab with me?"

The guard behind the investigator shook his head. "*Nyet.*"

Phillips looked at her again and nodded, as if to say she should go while she could. When she didn't move forward, her hovering guard gave her a slight shove that sent her into the hallway. There wasn't much else she could do for the investigator but hope and pray that nobody stood in his way of leaving the embassy.

The guard gripped her elbow and escorted her down the hall. If she hadn't dug her heels into the tile when she passed the restroom he would have marched her all the way to the exit.

Emily pulled free of the hand holding her arm and ducked into the bathroom. For a moment she thought the guard would follow her. When he didn't, she breathed a sigh as the door closed behind her.

What she had translated that day left her shaken.

The investigator had been hired to follow the ambassador's daughter and to find out where she had been going in Washington, DC. Apparently she'd had a number of unescorted clandestine assignations with a young man her father considered dangerous to his position as the Russian ambassador to the US. The investigator had stopped short of naming names but the look he'd exchanged with the ambassador had been clear. The ambassador knew who she was seeing.

The anger Emily had heard in the ambassador's voice led her to believe that he was livid enough to kill the young man and possibly even his daughter, Sachi.

Emily hadn't been altogether sure that she would make it out of the embassy alive. Though she'd never felt threatened before when she'd come to do translations within the Russian embassy, the anger in the ambassador's demeanor left her feeling anything but comfortable.

She quickly splashed water on her face and dried it with a paper towel. Then she straightened her shoulders and pushed through the door to exit the bathroom. As she emerged into the hallway a man wearing a press badge was being escorted into the embassy by two guards, each gripping one of the journalist's arms.

Emily was certain she'd seen the young man before but she couldn't quite place him at the moment.

The guard who had led her from the conference room grabbed her elbow and jerked her toward the exit. Emily was in just as much of a hurry to get out of the embassy as the guard was to get her out. She no longer felt safe.

As she worked her way to the door, a sense of urgency filled her. She had to get out of the building as quickly as possible. At the exit, she was stopped by another guard. The two burly men spoke in Russian, their speech so quick she only caught half of it. It appeared the guard at the door was reluctant to let her leave, whereas the other guard wanted her out as soon as possible. Finally her guard escort got her through the door and gave her a little push toward the gate leading off the embassy compound.

Hugging her purse against her body, and pulling her jacket tightly around her, Emily hurried for the gate. Again, she was stopped and questioned as to why she was at the embassy. She told them she had been there to translate. The guard at the gate waved her through and she was free.

Emily didn't look back. Instead she kept going, walking faster and faster until she was almost running down the street. She didn't stop running until she was several blocks from the embassy. Her heart beating fast, her breathing coming in ragged gasps, she finally stopped long enough to remember where she had parked her car. She had to backtrack to the lot where she had paid to park earlier that day.

As she crossed the street, a vehicle raced toward her without slowing. She quickened her pace but realized she wasn't going to make it across in time. The vehicle barreled forward, increasing speed rather than slowing, as if the driver didn't see her or had made her his target.

Emily dove for the sidewalk and rolled to the side. The vehicle rushing at her bumped up on the curb and nearly ran over her. If she hadn't rolled once more, it would have crushed her. The driver didn't stop to check that she was all right, but sped on, leaving her to pick herself up and dust the dirt off of her clothes.

A man reached down and gripped her elbow. "Are you all right?"

Emily nodded, her heart still pounding so hard she thought it might leap out of her chest. "I'm okay." She tried to get a look at the license plate to report the reckless driver, but the car didn't have a plate on the rear bumper.

Turning to the stranger, she said, "Thank you," and gave him a weak smile. Moving past him, Emily glanced down at the damage done to her trouser leg, which now sported a dirt stain and a tear, wondering what her knee looked like beneath it. It stung and hurt when she flexed it. She couldn't take care of it until she got home. After another glance around, she continued toward the car park. With nothing but a description of a dark sedan having nearly run her over, she gave up hope of turning in the man behind the wheel for reckless driving. Instead she slipped into her car, paid the parking lot attendant and drove out of downtown DC, putting distance between her and the Russian embassy.

Out of the downtown traffic, Emily drove onto a six-lane highway, crowded with people hurrying to get somewhere. A white van behind her sped up, swerved around her to the left and slammed into the side of her vehicle.

Emily held on to the steering wheel with a white-knuckled grip, struggling to keep from hitting the vehicle on her right. The driver on the other side of her honked as she crossed into his lane. Ahead of her, the van dodged in and out of traffic, leaving Emily behind before she could get a look at his license plate.

She slowed, unable to pull to the side of the road. The car behind her honked, the vehicles on either side boxing her in, keeping her moving steadily forward. She had no choice but to continue toward home. Shaken and paranoid, Emily held on tightly to the steering wheel, bracing for the next potential hit-and-run driver. What was wrong with people? Why were the drivers all bent on trying to run her over? After her encounter at the Russian embassy, she could swear they were deliberately attacking her. Or was she imagining it? Traffic was scary enough without aggressive people expressing their road rage with a three-thou-sand-pound deadly weapon.

By the time she drove into her neighbor-hood, Emily was tired, stressed and ready to kick her feet up and drink a glass of wine to calm her nerves.

The traffic light ahead turned green as she approached. She pressed the accelerator and entered the intersection.

A dark blue sedan shot out of the side road, completely ignoring the red light.

If Emily hadn't been ultra-aware of her envi-ronment, she wouldn't have reacted as quickly as she did. She slammed her foot on the gas pedal, pulling ahead just enough to avoid being T-boned by the other car. It missed hitting her rear bumper by a hair.

"What the heck?" Emily cried. She didn't slow, pushing past the speed limit to the next street. A glance in her rearview mirror showed the vehicle that had almost plowed into her was turning in the middle of the intersection, aim-ing toward her.

After this third vehicular incident, Emily got a clue. Instead of driving straight to her apartment she drove past her complex, watching closely in her rearview mirror as the dark sedan followed.

She turned at the next corner and the trailing car continued on straight. She breathed a sigh of relief and headed toward her apartment, keeping an eye on the rearview mirror. From all she could tell, no one was following her. She made a circuitous trip around the block before she pulled into the parking lot of her building.

Her heart still pounding, Emily slowed her vehicle and started to turn into her usual parking space.

Although it was still a part of a normal workday, there were several cars in the lot, most of which were empty. When she spotted the dark blue sedan, Emily's heart did a flip-flop.

The windows were too darkly tinted to see inside.

A tightening in the pit of Emily's stomach made her pause before parking. Her heart sped up as she lifted her foot off of the brake and applied it to the accelerator. Instead of turning into her parking space, she whipped through the lot and out the other end of the apartment complex.

As she turned back out onto the road, she glanced into her rearview mirror and saw again the dark sedan pulling out of the parking lot, following her. She raced to the next street and turned.

The blue sedan stayed right on her tail.

Not knowing what to do, she chose a busy thoroughfare and rushed out into the open, hoping and praying the traffic would help put some distance between her and the sedan. Whipping in and out of traffic and dodging vehicles, Emily did manage to put distance between her and her tail. When she thought she'd lost him, she called her friend Grace, using her car's Bluetooth setup.

Grace answered on the first ring. "Hi, Emily, how's it going?"

"I think I'm in trouble," she said, her voice wobbling.

"What kind of trouble?" Grace's voice was sharp, filled with concern.

"I'm not sure," Emily said. "I think I'm being followed, and drivers have tried to run me off the road a couple of times in the past hour. I—I can't go home."

"Try to stay calm. You know you called the right person," Grace said. "Charlie's guys will help. Where are you now?"

Emily glanced around, for the first time aware that she hadn't headed anywhere in particular, just away from trouble. "I'm on 395. I don't know where," she said. "Wait, there's an exit sign." She gave Grace her location and then glanced in her mirror once more. "Crap! There he is again," she said.

"I'm going to text you a map coordinate," Grace said. "It's the address of my new employer. Go straight there, I'll have somebody meet you at the gate."

A beep sounded on her cell phone. Emily took her eyes off the road long enough to select the coordinates for her map on her phone to follow. She'd slowed just enough that the dark sedan behind her was quickly catching up. While her map application calculated the directions, she again weaved in and out of traffic, trying to lose her tail.

"Stay on the phone with me, Emily," Grace said. "I have a team of people here at Charlie's place. They can help you. You just have to get here."

"I'll do the best I can," Emily promised.

She thought she'd been doing well and had lost her tail when she'd finally pulled off the main parkway onto a smaller road. But as soon as the traffic thinned, she looked behind her.

The dark-tinted vehicle was there and speeding up, closing in on her. The road she traveled now was lined with gated driveways. Besides the gates and the driveways, there was nothing else around. No cars. No people. Just her and the sedan that was quickly catching up.

"Are you still with me, Emily?" Grace asked.

"I'm here," she said. This time when she glanced in her rearview mirror the vehicle behind her was racing toward her back bumper. Emily pressed her foot to the accelerator, shooting her little car forward. Her speed increased from fifty to sixty to seventy miles per hour. A caution sign on the side of the road indicated an upcoming curve, with a recommended speed of twenty-five miles per hour.

Afraid the vehicle behind her would rearend her and send her flying off the road, Emily didn't dare slow down. She gripped the steering wheel and raced into the curve at breakneck speed. As she navigated the radius, the rear end of her vehicle fishtailed and swung around. She almost went into a 360-degree spin, was able to correct her direction, but not soon enough to avoid the vehicle following her.

The car behind her slammed into her left rear fender, sending her back into the spin.

Out of her control, her car slid toward the edge of the road.

Emily squealed and held tight to the steering wheel as her vehicle bumped onto the shoulder, down into a ditch and up an embankment, slamming into a fence post. Upon impact, the airbags deployed, forcing her back against her seat, stunning her for a few precious seconds. Emily rubbed the dust out of her eyes and looked around. The fine powder of the airbag coated her skin and clothes and the dash of the vehicle.

In her rearview mirror, she could see the road behind her and the dark sedan parked at the edge. A man dressed in black, with a black ski mask pulled over his head, got out of the driver's side and stood on the shoulder, staring down at her vehicle.

Emily didn't move, praying her attacker would think she was unconscious and leave.

When he moved toward her, she couldn't sit still, she had to get away.

Emily shifted her vehicle into Reverse and hit the accelerator. The rear tires spun, gaining no traction. She couldn't go forward because of the fence post. She tried turning the steering wheel sharply to the left and hit the accelerator again. The back tire spun, shooting mud up behind her, but the vehicle didn't budge.

"What's happening, Emily?" Grace's voice said over the phone. "What was that noise? Are you okay?"

"No, no, I'm not. I've crashed," Emily managed to croak out as she struggled with what to do. "I have to… I'm getting out…" She couldn't waste time talking. Escape was her only option.

The man on the side of the road scrambled down into the ditch, moving purposefully toward her. Emily tried to open her door to get out, but the door was jammed. She fumbled with the catch on her seat belt and finally got it loose.

Her pulse pounding loudly against her eardrums, Emily crawled across the console to the other side of the vehicle and pulled the door handle. When the door swung open, she fell out onto the ground, rolled onto her side, bunched her feet and knees up beneath her and rose.

When she raised her head above the car, she could see the man in black standing there, his hand rising, a gun held in his grip.

Emily's heart leaped to her throat. She ducked back down behind the car as a shot rang out. Glass shattered, raining down from the window above her as Emily lay flat against the earth. The scent of gasoline, tire rubber and the mud beneath her nose filled her senses. But she couldn't lie there for long. If her pursuer came any closer, he could easily pick her off with his handgun.

Unwilling to die that day, Emily rose onto her hands and knees. Keeping low to the ground, she crawled for the fence, slipped beneath the bottom rail and continued on toward the trees, praying she could find a place to hide until the crazy man following her gave up and went away. Or until Grace's friends arrived to rescue her.

Chapter Two

Frank "Mustang" Ford's cell phone rang through to the Bluetooth in his truck. Declan O'Neill's name appeared on the dash screen.

Mustang thumbed the button on his steering wheel to answer. "What's up, Declan?"

"Are you on your way to the Halverson Estate?"

"Roger," he confirmed. "Five miles away. Why? Need me to stop and pick up some milk or bread?" He chuckled.

"No. I have a mission for you."

"Really?" Mustang sat straighter. "Must be a short deadline if you can't wait until I get to Charlie's place."

"It is," Declan said, his tone clipped. "Be on the lookout for a red Toyota Camry. Grace's friend is en route to Charlie's and has a tail following her. She reported three vehicular attacks since leaving the DC area. She might be in trouble."

"I'll keep an eye out for her. The road out this way appears pretty deserted."

"Then it shouldn't be hard to find her. Let us know when you catch up to her."

"Roger." As he increased his speed, Mustang gripped the steering wheel a little tighter.

A mile or more later a yellow caution sign indicated a sharp curve ahead. Mustang applied his brakes, his gaze scanning the sides of the road and the ditches. If someone was trying to harm Grace's friend, running her off the road in the middle of a curve was the perfect place to do it. Dusk was settling in, causing shadows to merge, making it more difficult for Mustang to distinguish between shadows and objects on the sides of the road.

As soon as he entered the sweeping curve, he spied a dark vehicle parked barely off the shoulder. The driver's-side door hung open and, as far as Mustang could tell, no one was inside or around the vehicle. He slowed, pulled over to the side of the road and off onto the shoulder, giving the vehicle in front of him plenty of space. He shifted into Park, grabbed his flashlight from the center console and pulled his handgun from the shoulder holster beneath his jacket.

Mustang slipped down out of his truck and closed the door quietly. As he rounded the hood and edged toward the dark sedan he spied another vehicle on the other side of the ditch crashed against a fence pole. It, too, seemed abandoned and, from what he could tell, it was red. The front bumper was smashed into the fence post and the driver's-side window was shattered with what looked like a bullet hole at the exact position that would have hit the driver, had the driver been sitting in the seat.

Adrenaline shot through Mustang's veins. Crouching low, he eased toward the abandoned vehicles, dropped down into the ditch and climbed up the embankment to the disabled vehicle where he discovered the passenger door was open. He prayed that whoever had been in the car had escaped. All he could assume at the moment was that whoever had arrived in the dark sedan had been the one to run the other vehicle off the road and to fire the shot that had put the hole in the driver's-side window. That led Mustang to believe the driver of the disabled vehicle was on the run, being chased now by whoever had attacked her.

With his gun held at the ready, he pointed his flashlight with his other hand into the front seat of the disabled vehicle. He was glad to discover there was no blood on the seats or the dash. The airbags had deployed and the vehicle was empty, meaning the driver had escaped.

But how long would she last on the run from somebody trying to kill her with a gun? She could be injured. The question was, what direction had she gone in?

He tried to think like a person running from somebody determined to kill her. She would have made for the safety and concealment of the tree line. That meant that she would have slipped beneath the fence into the forest. She might only have seconds before her pursuer caught up to her.

Mustang ran the rest of the way up the embankment, braced his hand on a fence rail and vaulted over the metal railing. As his feet hit the ground, a shot rang out. He raced in the direction he thought the sound had come from, determined to reach the woman before her attacker finished her off. He hoped he wasn't too late.

Mustang raced as fast as he could, leaping over branches, pushing past bushes and trees. His muscles strained and his lungs burned, and still he didn't see anyone ahead of him.

It had been dusk when he'd pulled to the side of the road. Within the canopy of the trees, darkness had descended. He couldn't see every little branch and tripped over one. He got up and kept moving, arriving finally at the edge of a glen where a little bit of dusk light illuminated a dark figure standing over a lump on the ground. From the man's silhouette, Mustang could tell he was pointing a gun at the figure on the ground. Mustang raised his weapon and fired. The dark figure ducked. When he straightened, he pulled the person up from the ground and held her in front of him.

"Come another step closer and I will shoot her," a voice said in a thick Russian accent.

Mustang took cover behind a tree. "You shoot her and I'll hunt you down and kill you. I will show you no mercy."

Though he spoke with force, Mustang could not help the shaky feeling he felt inside. What he witnessed before him was so similar to the last operation he and his team had conducted in Afghanistan. In that scenario, their bogey had used the bride in a wedding couple as the shield to get him out of a village. That Taliban leader's ploy and Mustang's team decision to spare the bride had cost them all their careers in the marines. And, as had been the case then, he couldn't take the shot now. If he attempted to kill the bad guy, he'd have to go through the body of an innocent victim.

"Okay. I won't shoot," Mustang shouted. "But I reiterate, if you kill the woman, I *will* kill you. And I will make certain that you suffer in the process of dying."

The man holding the hostage inched backward, dragging the woman with him. He made a wide circle, heading back in the direction of the road and the vehicles abandoned there.

Mustang had no recourse but to wait for the man to pass him and continue on his path to the road. At one point Mustang thought he heard the woman sob and, possibly, a softly spoken plea. *Help me.* His heart contracted, squeezing tightly in his chest. He vowed to himself that he'd get her out of her attacker's grasp.

Mustang followed, keeping a safe distance but close enough that he could see what was going on in the shadowy darkness of late dusk. At one point he got too near.

"Do not come closer," the attacker said. He fired a shot.

Mustang ducked low and behind a tree.

Thankfully the woman remained on her feet, still dragged alongside her kidnapper. They closed the distance between them and the vehicles on the side of the road.

Mustang knew he had to stop the kidnapper before he got the woman into the car. If he had been bent on running her off the road and shooting at her inside her vehicle, he would kill her as soon as he got her away. Mustang couldn't let that happen. He had to stop the kidnapper.

Mustang eased through the woods, moving shadow to shadow, inching closer as quietly as he could. When the other two reached the fence, Mustang knew he had to make his move. The kidnapper shoved the woman to the ground and said something to her in Russian. She rolled beneath the fence.

"My finger is on the trigger," the Russian called out. "If you shoot me. I shoot the woman. I might die, but the woman will die, as well."

With the man in his sights, Mustang hesitated.

The woman, who had managed to get beneath the fence, kicked out a foot, catching her kidnapper in the shin with a hard smack.

Mustang took his chance and pulled the trigger at the same time the Russian yelled and bent over.

The woman on the ground rolled and kept rolling past the fence and down the embankment, out of sight of Mustang. Her attacker climbed over the top of the fence and dropped down on the other side.

Mustang left the concealment of the tree and raced for the fence, vaulting over and landing on the other side. He immediately dropped to his belly on the ground.

A shot rang out.

The woman had managed to roll to the bottom of the ditch, get up and start running from the Russian.

Her attacker rose and pointed his weapon at her.

Mustang aimed and fired, hitting the man's hand, knocking the gun from his grip.

Clutching his injured hand to his chest, the Russian ran for the dark sedan on the roadside.

Mustang glanced from the assailant to the woman. He wanted to stop the Russian from making another attempt on the woman's life. But first he needed to ascertain what injuries the woman might have sustained. Headlights shone in the curve on the road above as the dark sedan sped away with the Russian inside. Meanwhile the woman hadn't stopped. She kept running, tripping over bushes and bramble in the ditch. If she didn't stop soon she'd injure herself even more.

"Mustang," a man shouted. "You out there?"

Mustang breathed a sigh of relief at the sound of Declan's voice.

"Do you need help?" Declan called out.

"Call 9-1-1, get an ambulance out here." Mustang didn't wait for Declan's response. He raced after the woman scrabbling through the ditch. Because of the recent rain the ditch contained pools of standing water and mushy soil.

The woman stumbled and fell into the mud.

Mustang splashed through the water. "Hey!"

His shout seemed to galvanize her and she pushed to her feet and resumed running. Her breathing coming in ragged gasps and sobs.

Mustang increased his speed.

Apparently the woman didn't realize that he was one of the good guys. She had to be so frightened that she was beyond reason. She struggled up the incline toward the road. If Mustang didn't catch up to her soon, she could be hit by an oncoming vehicle as soon as she emerged from the ditch.

The headlights shining on the road above made Mustang kick up his pace and he charged after the woman. Just before she reached the road, he caught her with a flying tackle, sending her sprawling onto the gravel. He pulled her beneath him and rolled her to the side, away from the oncoming car. After the vehicle had passed, he pushed up on his arms and stared down into the shadowy face of the woman. Her features were blurred in the looming darkness, but he could tell she had a scrape on her chin and her eyes were wide and frightened.

She fought, kicking and screaming something in Russian.

Mustang used the weight of his body to hold her against the ground.

When he didn't shift off her, she switched to English. "Let go of me."

Mustang pinned her wrists to the ground to keep her from scratching his eyes out. "Hey, lady. I'm just here to help you."

Her struggle slowed and finally came to a halt. She stared up at him. "If you're here to help me, let me go," she said.

He chuckled. "Sweetheart, I'll let you go when I'm sure you're not gonna run out into the traffic."

She dragged in a long, shaky breath and let it out. "I promise, I won't run out into the traffic. And I'm not your sweetheart."

For a long moment Mustang stared down into her face, wishing he could see the color of her eyes in the darkness. Finally he sighed and rolled over, releasing her wrists. "Okay. But I'll tackle you again if you try to get out onto the highway."

She sat up, rubbing her wrists where he'd held them so tightly.

"Grace sent us," Mustang said.

The woman's head jerked up and she stared into his eyes. "Are you some of Charlie's men?"

"If you mean do I work for Charlie Halverson, then yes." Mustang pushed to his feet and extended his hand.

She hesitated a moment before placing her hand in his and letting him pull her to her feet.

"Are you okay?" His gaze raked her body from head to toe, his eyes straining in the darkness. He'd lost the flashlight in his chase to catch her.

She nodded. "I think so. A little banged up and bruised from the car wreck and from being tackled."

"Sorry about that," Mustang said.

A smile quirked at the corners of her lips. "I guess I should thank you for keeping me safe from running out into the middle of the road."

Footsteps sounded on the pavement behind the woman. Declan raced toward them. "Mustang? Emily?" He ground to a halt and shook his head. "An ambulance is on the way. And I called the sheriff's department and the police department and have them looking out for a dark sedan with no license plate."

Mustang shook his head. "The dude will be long gone before anybody gets out here."

Declan stepped up to Emily and held out his hand. "Grace sent us. You must be Emily."

The woman took his hand and nodded. "I'm Emily," she said softly. "Thank you for coming to my rescue."

Declan chuckled and tipped his head at Mustang. "You'll have to thank Mustang. He's the one who came to your rescue."

She raised her eyebrows and shot a glance toward Mustang. "Mustang? Is that your real name or is that a call sign?"

"Call sign," Mustang answered. "Frank Ford." He held out his hand and she took it, giving it a firm shake before releasing it and rubbing her hand on the side of her leg.

The wailing of a siren brought all three heads up at once. Lights blinked around the corner and an ambulance came to a stop beside Mustang's truck. The EMT crew leaped out of their rig and converged on Emily.

She held up her hands and backed away. "I'm okay," she insisted.

Mustang touched her shoulder. "Let them look you over. Even if it doesn't make you feel better, it will make me feel better," he said and stepped back to let the EMT crew get to Emily.

Declan fell in beside Mustang. "Did you get a look at the guy who attacked her?"

Mustang shook his head. "No, it was dark, and the guy wore a ski mask." He stared in the direction the dark sedan had gone. "However, the man had a Russian accent."

Declan's brows rose. "Russian, aye."

Mustang shrugged. "Not that I speak Russian. But it sounded like it to me, and Emily apparently can speak Russian because she said something in Russian when I tackled her."

Declan chuckled. "You tackled her?"

With a frown, Mustang nodded. "I had to, to stop her from running out in the road."

Declan shook his head. "That's no way to make a new friend."

Mustang snorted. "I wasn't trying to make a friend. I was trying to save her from getting run over."

Declan clapped a hand to Mustang's shoulder. "Well, that will make Grace happy. She was worried about Emily."

When the EMTs brought out a stretcher, they were stopped by an emphatic, *No!*

Emily shrugged out of the hands of one of the technicians. "I'm okay, I'm telling you."

"Ma'am, being in a car wreck, and having the airbags deploy, can cause concussion. We'd feel better if you came to the hospital and had one of the doctors look you over."

Emily shook her head. "At no time was I unconscious."

"You don't have to be unconscious to have suffered a concussion." The EMT gripped her arm. "Please, ma'am, let us take care of you."

She shook off his hand and backed away. "I'm okay and I can take care of myself." She looked around, her gaze catching Mustang's.

"If I've suffered any injuries, my friends will make sure that I get to a hospital on time. Won't you?" She directed her challenge at Declan.

Declan chuckled. "We'll get her to the nearest hospital if she starts showing any signs of deteriorating health."

The technician shrugged. "Have it your way." He closed his kit and loaded it into the emergency vehicle. The two other technicians who'd gotten the stretcher out put it into the back of the ambulance and eventually the three of them drove away.

Emily turned and stared at the wreckage of her car. "I don't suppose I'm going to get that out of the ditch anytime soon," she said.

Again Declan chuckled. "No. The only thing that's going to get that vehicle out of the ditch is a tow truck."

Emily sighed and turned to Declan and Mustang. "I take it you're my ride."

Declan nodded. "However, you do have a choice between riding with me—" he tipped his head toward Mustang "—or with Mustang."

Emily's eyes narrowed as she stared from Mustang to Declan and back.

Mustang found himself holding his breath. He didn't know why, and he didn't know the woman, but he wanted her to choose him.

Though she was soaked with the equivalent of swamp water, he had come this far to save her. He didn't want to let it end there.

For several seconds Emily chewed on her bottom lip. Then she drew in a breath, let it go on a sigh and nodded at Mustang. "I'll ride with Mustang," she said softly.

"Well then, let's get you to Charlie's place. It's not too far down the road. That way you can get out of those cold, wet clothes. It's starting to get chilly outside," Declan said.

Emily nodded, a shiver shaking her frame.

Declan grinned. "I'll see you there." He spun on his heels and hurried toward his truck.

When Mustang tried to steer her toward his truck, Emily dug her heels into the pavement. "I can't leave my purse and keys in the car." She started toward the wrecked vehicle.

"I'll get them," Mustang insisted. "Stay here."

He dropped down into the ditch and found his way into the damaged vehicle. After pulling the keys from the ignition, he took longer than he wanted to find the purse. Finally, he had what he needed and returned to Emily's side.

Mustang handed her the purse and keys, gripped her elbow and led her to the passenger side of his pickup. He opened the door to assist her into the seat.

She put her foot on the running board and it slipped, causing her to fall back into Mustang's arms.

He held her until she had her feet firmly on the ground again. "You all right?"

She nodded. Color rose up her neck and into her cheeks. She reached this time for the handle inside the cab of the truck and helped pull herself up into the passenger seat.

Once Emily was settled, Mustang reached around her and clicked the shoulder strap of the seat belt across her lap. As he retracted his elbow, it brushed gently across her breast and he quickly mumbled an apology. A blast of electricity shot through him.

Emily's breath hitched, as if she'd had a similar experience.

Mustang jerked his arm back and stepped away from the side of the truck, slamming the door firmly. He rounded the front of the vehicle and climbed into the driver's seat. Without another word, he started the engine and pulled out onto the road. The shock he'd felt had to have been static electricity. There could be no other explanation. There was no way he'd felt a connection with the cold, wet woman who'd showed a remarkable amount of spirit and courage in her escape from her captor. Mustang barely knew the woman.

Chapter Three

They'd gone maybe a little more than a mile when Mustang pulled off at a large, impressive stone wall and wrought-iron gate. Declan's truck had just pulled through onto the estate and he waved his hand out the window for them to follow.

Mustang drove through and the gate closed slowly behind them.

Emily had heard Grace talk about her new employer, Charlie, or Charlotte Halverson, the widow of a wealthy philanthropist. Grace had gone on and on about the beautiful estate and how kind and caring her employer was to her collection of employees.

Having been the most recent recipient of Charlie's kindness, Emily was anxious to meet the woman. If Charlie had not sent Mustang out to help, Emily was absolutely certain she would not be alive to appreciate the beauty of Charlie's estate at that moment.

She glanced toward the man beside her, studying him in the light from the dash.

He was tall, with broad shoulders and a ruggedly handsome face. Something about his stoic countenance tugged deeply at Emily's insides. Or perhaps she was just grateful he'd arrived when he had and saved her from being shot. Either way, she felt closer to this man than any other stranger she had ever met.

Chills rippled through Emily. She fought to keep her teeth from chattering. Her clothes were damp, and she smelled like swamp water, but she couldn't help that.

"S-s-so you work for Charlie?" she asked.

Mustang gave a curt nod. "Yeah."

"W-w-what do you do for her?" Emily wrapped her hands around her arms and shivered in her seat.

He adjusted the thermostat on the dash to make it blow blessedly warm air. "She hired Declan and then he brought the rest of our team on board. I guess you could say we are kind of a security agency."

"Does the agency have a name?" Emily asked.

Mustang smiled. "Declan's Defenders."

"So, Declan is your leader?" Emily asked.

Mustang nodded. "He was our team lead before. It just seemed natural for him to be lead of Declan's Defenders."

"Before?" Emily stared across the console at the man driving.

Mustang's jaw tightened. "We were in the marines together."

Emily nodded silently. She should have recognized his military bearing. The man didn't have an ounce of flab or fat on him. And when he stood, he held himself straight, shoulders back and head held high, the countenance and bearing of someone who had been in the military, living under strict rules and guidelines.

Mustang shot a glance her way. "So what did you do to piss someone off enough that they want to kill you?"

Emily shook her head. "I have no idea," she said.

"I seriously doubt it was a case of road rage," Mustang noted.

Emily snorted. "Well, if it was road rage, he did a good job of it. He ran me off the road."

"And chased you down with a gun." Mustang's brows dipped. "If I'm not mistaken, that man spoke Russian. And when I tackled you, you spoke in Russian, as well. What's up with that?"

Emily ran a hand through her hair and stared out the window beside her. "I'm a Russian interpreter. No, I'm not Russian, I'm American, but I studied Russian in high school and college. I also studied abroad in Moscow for a semester. Now I teach Russian at Georgetown and I translate for people who speak Russian."

"Was the guy who tried to kill you one of the clients you translated for?"

Emily pressed her lips together. "You know as much as I do. The man wore a ski mask. I couldn't tell you if he was one of my clients." A shiver shook Emily so hard her teeth rattled.

Mustang glanced at her again. "You're cold."

She nodded.

"Sorry, I should have given you this earlier." He reached over the back of the seat, grabbed a blanket and threw it across her lap. "Wrap yourself in that. You need to warm up."

Emily picked at the blanket. "I hate to get it all wet and smelly."

"Don't worry about it. It'll wash."

Mustang followed Declan's taillights as they twisted and turned on the tree-lined road leading to Charlotte Halverson's massive mansion.

Emily wrapped the blanket around her lap, thankful for the warmth. She would be sure to wash and return it when she got back to her apartment. Then she'd begin the hassle of getting her car repaired or replaced. In the meantime she was dependent on Charlotte Halverson and Declan's Defenders to get her around. And she was thankful they'd come through for her when she'd needed them.

As they pulled up in front of the three-story mansion with its many gables and arches, several men descended the marble staircase from the front door. Three women followed, one of whom Emily recognized as Grace. And the other, her friend Riley. The front porch lights shone down on the third woman's gray hair. That had to be Charlotte Halverson. Emily had seen pictures of her in the news and in the papers.

Mustang pulled to a stop and shifted into Park. Before he could get out and around to the other side of the truck, the door opened and Declan held out his hand for her.

Emily pushed the blanket off her lap and accepted the assistance to get down from the truck.

Grace, the first woman to reach her, wrapped her in her arms. "Oh, sweetie, I'm so sorry this happened to you."

"I'm okay. Mustang got there in time." Emily briefly hugged her back and then pulled away. "Sorry. I'm soaked and I'm sure I smell."

Grace's brow furrowed as she held Emily at arm's length and raked her gaze over her from head to toe. "What happened?"

"We'll fill you all in when Emily's had a chance to get out of those damp clothes," Mustang said.

"Right." Grace hooked Emily's arm. "We'll find you something to wear. I have enough clothes here, I might as well move in permanently."

The gray-haired woman stepped forward. "I've left an open invitation for you and Declan to take the west wing."

Grace smiled at her employer. "Charlie, this is my friend, Emily. Emily, meet Charlotte Halverson, my new boss."

Emily held out her hand. "Nice to m-meet y-you," she said, her teeth rattling. "And th-thank y-you."

"Oh, pish." Charlie took Emily's hand and frowned. "Your hands are like ice. Inside. Now." She grabbed Emily's other elbow and marched her up the steps. The door opened as if automatically.

Once inside, Emily saw a man dressed in a suit, holding the door handle, standing at attention.

"That's Arnold, my butler," Charlie said. "Don't let him intimidate you. I can't get him to wear anything but a suit." She winked at Arnold as she passed him. "But I can't live without him, so he gets his way more often than not. Isn't that right, Arnold?"

"Yes, Mrs. Halverson." Arnold gave her a slight bow.

"Charlie. I've told you to call me Charlie."

Without changing his expression the butler nodded. "Yes, ma'am."

Charlie shook her head and gave a wry grin to Emily. "Please, call me Charlie. Mrs. Halverson was my husband's mother."

Emily forced a smile past her chattering teeth. "Charlie," she repeated softly.

"Mrs. Halverson, would you like me to escort your guest to a bedroom?" Albert asked in his flat, expressionless tone.

Charlie waved a hand. "No need. Grace and I will take her." She charged across a smooth white-marble foyer and started up the stairs.

Feeling like she was being dragged along by a freight train, Emily looked back over her shoulder, her gaze searching for and finding Mustang's.

"I'll be here when you get cleaned up," he said.

She gave him a quick smile and followed Charlie up the stairs, Grace bringing up the rear. Why she should be relieved Mustang was staying, she didn't know. Surrounded by Grace and Charlie, Emily should feel reassured. However she'd never had a man point a gun at her, much less discharge it in an attempt to kill her.

Mustang had been the one to save her. She felt confident that if her attacker tried again to kill her, Mustang would keep him from succeeding. Knowing he was sticking around made her feel much better.

Although Emily had been in a number of posh hotels and opulent embassies, she'd never been inside a multimillionaire's mansion. Everywhere she looked, what appeared to be priceless objects were perched on tables, in alcoves and hung on the walls. She imagined she could pay her rent for a year with even one of the vases or paintings.

Charlie turned right at the top of the staircase. "You can stay in the Banyan Room while you're here."

"Thank you. But as soon as I can, I'd like to return to my apartment."

Grace grabbed Emily's arm. "Sweetie, you can't go back to your apartment as long as that maniac is still out there."

Charlie nodded. "Agreed. And I have plenty of empty rooms. You'll stay here." Her tone didn't allow for argument.

But Emily couldn't put her life on hold. "I have a job. I work at the university. I have students to teach."

Charlie shook her head. "Honey, you can't teach if you're dead."

A lead weight settled at the pit of Emily's belly.

"And if you show up at the university, who's to say your attacker won't show up, as well?" Grace added. "You would be putting your students at risk of being caught in the crossfire."

The lead weight twisted in Emily's gut. They were right. "But I can't hide here forever. I have bills to pay."

"Then we'll have to figure out who attacked you."

"You can't do it on your own. I'm the only one who knows my life. I won't stand by and let others put themselves at risk for me."

"Then I'll assign one of Declan's Defenders to protect you and help you figure out who has it in for you." Charlie crossed her arms over her chest. "In the meantime, you need a safe place to sleep. Your apartment isn't that place. I have enough security wired into this estate, you won't have to worry about anyone getting in."

Emily smiled and hugged Charlie. "Thank you. If you hadn't sent Mustang to help me, I wouldn't even be here to have this conversation."

"Any one of Declan's Defenders would have

done the same. But since Mustang saved your life, he now has a vested interest in keeping you alive." Charlie waved toward the room. "While you get cleaned up, I'll have a word with Declan about assigning Mustang to protect you."

Warmth spread through Emily's body, loosening the knot in her stomach. Despite her desire to get back to work, she didn't want to put herself or her students in danger.

Charlie left Emily and Grace and headed for the staircase.

Grace chuckled. "Charlie is a force to be reckoned with."

"Yes, she is," Emily agreed.

"But she has a heart of gold and would do anything for you." Grace touched Emily's shoulder, guiding her to the other side of the bedroom where a door led to an attached bathroom. "While you get a shower, I'll gather some of my clothes."

Tears filled Emily's eyes. "Thank you, Grace. You saved my life."

Grace laughed. "I didn't save your life. Mustang did."

"Because you had him sent to me." A tear slipped down her cheek. "I don't think I've ever been more afraid in my life."

"Honey, I know what you mean," Grace

said, her voice tight, her lips pressing together briefly. "I've been there."

Emily nodded. "Yes, you were. Back when Riley went missing."

"Declan was there when I needed him. He and his men went to bat for me, and for Riley when things got sticky for her, too. They'll help you. And Mustang's a good man. He'll take care of you."

"I want to say I don't need anyone to take care of me but…" A shiver shook her wet frame. "Apparently I do. I've never had a man shoot at me or hold a gun to my head."

"Oh, sweetie." Grace pulled Emily's bedraggled form into her arms. "I'm sorry you had to go through that. Hopefully the team can help figure out who did this to you and why." She turned Emily and gave her a gentle shove in the direction of the bathroom. "For now, get cleaned up and warm. Everything will look better once you are."

"Thank you, Grace." Emily entered the bathroom and closed the door behind her, leaning against it to keep from falling. Another shiver shook her, and another, until her entire body quaked with the tremors. She knew it was shock setting in. If she didn't get into a warm shower soon, she didn't know what would happen. She could pass out or die from hypothermia. After Mustang went to the effort of saving her, that would be a crappy way to repay him.

She pushed away from the door and took stock of the beautiful bathroom. Six of her apartment bathrooms could fit in the space. White quartz counters and sinks shone, sparkling clean. A large bathtub invited the guest to fill it full of warm water, bath salts and oils. Bypassing the tub, Emily walked to the shower, turned on the faucet and waited for the water to warm.

Her hands shook as she stripped out of her wet clothing and dropped the garments to the smooth, tiled floor.

When the water was warmer than her skin, she stepped beneath it and let it run over her head, shoulders and the length of her body. As the heat chased away the chills, she squirted a liberal amount of shampoo into her palm and smoothed it over her hair, digging her fingers in, determined to wash away the smell of stagnant water.

Emily leaned her head back, closed her eyes and let the water sluice over her. As the soap bubbles slid down over her breasts, a sudden image intruded on her thoughts. An erotic scene, completely at odds with the suspenseful one she'd just lived through. Maybe it was a coping mechanism, but she couldn't get the thought out of her head. One of Mustang rubbing his hands together to create lather and smoothing them all over her body.

Shocked by her own imagination, Emily opened her eyes and took in a deep, steadying breath. She had to be having some kind of post-traumatic lust for the man who'd saved her. She didn't know Mustang from Adam. He could be married, for all she knew. Her heart pounded against her ribs. She could be having lustful thoughts over a married man.

Grabbing the bottle of body wash, she completed her shower in record time, scrubbing every inch of her skin to remove traces of mud and ditch water.

When she emerged from the shower, she found a neat stack of clothing on the counter and a fluffy white towel.

She smiled at Grace's thoughtfulness.

Her lips turned down as she dressed. How could she face Mustang when she'd just been thinking about him naked?

Chapter Four

Mustang paced the floor of one of the spacious living rooms in Charlie's mansion. He'd been inside the home a number of times since going to work for the rich widow. Still, he didn't feel comfortable surrounded by the opulence millions of dollars could afford to buy. He preferred the comfort of his own little house. The one he'd purchased since landing the job with Declan's Defenders.

In all of the years he'd been on active duty, he'd never established roots in any one place. Since signing on with his brothers in arms to a decent job with a steady income and benefits, he'd decided it was time.

His friends had given him a hard time about having a home without a partner. Mustang didn't care. It was his, and he could do anything he wanted with it. If he wanted to paint the walls purple with green polka dots, he could. He didn't have to ask permission of a landlord or the government.

Though he'd prefer to be at his own house, he wasn't about to leave until he knew Emily was safe. Even then, he didn't want to leave without her. After saving her life, he felt responsible for her. Since her attacker had gotten away, she couldn't be one hundred percent safe.

"What do you know about Emily?" Mustang asked Declan.

"Only that she's a friend of Grace's, works at a university teaching Russian and performs as an interpreter when needed." Declan shrugged. "I got all of that today when Grace told me Emily was in trouble."

Mustang made another pass of the living room, feeling like a caged lion ready to bust out and roar. "Grace didn't say anything about her work? Anything or anyone who might have it in for her?"

Declan shook his head. "Nothing."

Stopping in front of a massive fireplace, Mustang ran a hand through his hair. "I should have killed the bastard."

"And if you'd gone after him, you'd have left Emily unprotected." Declan clapped a hand on Mustang's shoulder. "You did the right thing."

"Oh, good." Charlie entered the living room and smiled at Mustang. "I'm glad you stayed."

Declan stepped forward. "How's Emily?"

Mustang hung back, wanting to know the answer and barely willing to wait for Charlie's response.

"She's okay," Charlie said. "Shaken but okay."

Mustang released a silent sigh. He'd worried she might have had injuries not readily apparent.

"She's okay for now, anyway." Charlie directed her gaze at Declan and then Mustang. "However, I'm concerned."

"So are we," Declan responded. "Emily needs someone protecting her at all times, until her attacker can be found and dealt with."

Charlie smiled. "I agree. Who from your team do you suggest?"

Mustang's heart pounded against his ribs as he stepped forward. "I'll do it."

A frown pulled at Charlie's brow. "Are you sure? It will mean being with her 24/7."

"He's young, single and has the skills needed to protect Emily," Declan said.

The corners of Charlie's lips quirked. "Are you sure there's not someone more suited than Mustang?"

"She's mine," Mustang blurted. "I mean, I've already saved her life once. I feel it's my duty to protect her and continue to keep her safe."

Charlie grinned. "I was hoping you'd feel

that way. I think she will feel most comfortable with you, for just that reason."

Declan nodded. "I agree. The rest of my men will be backup when not otherwise engaged."

"Good." Charlie raised an eyebrow. "Then, Mustang, you'll be staying here until further notice. You'll be in the room next to Emily's."

"What?" Mustang frowned. "Why here?"

"Unless you or Emily have an airtight security system at your homes, she will not be as safe as she can be here."

"She's right," Declan interjected. "I've gone over all the security devices, cameras and fences. No one will get in without setting off an alarm and having half a dozen guards swarming all over them."

"Can you or Emily top that?" Charlie tilted her head. "If so, by all means. Otherwise, I have plenty of room, as Grace and Declan can attest to."

Mustang pressed his lips together. So much for enjoying his own home. But until Emily's attacker was apprehended and Emily was safe to go about her own life again, Mustang would do what it took to be close enough to protect her. "I'm in."

"Do you need to go back to your home to collect clothing and toiletries?" Charlie asked.

He shook his head. "I keep a go-bag in my

truck for emergencies. I can get by on what I have stashed in it."

"Smart man." Charlie clapped her hands together. "Now that we've settled who's protecting Emily, I'll make sure the chef increases the number of plates to serve at dinner." Charlie left the room.

Mustang's head spun.

Declan chuckled. "Charlie doesn't give anyone a chance to say no." His smile faded. "But seriously, man, are you good to go with this?"

Mustang nodded. "I'm good."

"Then get your gear and meet me and some of the others in the basement conference room. I'll have Grace and Emily join us when they're ready."

Mustang headed for the front entrance.

"Pardon me, sir." Arnold, the butler, stood in front of the door. "Are you the owner of the truck that had been parked out front?"

"I'm one of them. Declan's is the other," Mustang replied.

"I hope you don't mind, but I took the liberty of parking both of them in the rear garage."

"Okay." Mustang turned. "Could you point me in the right direction? I need to collect my gear bag."

"I'll show you, sir." Arnold stepped forward, his posture impeccable, his gate measured. He moved swiftly as he led Mustang through the foyer, past a living area, a study and the massive kitchen. They finally reached a back entrance. The butler paused long enough to hold open the door for Mustang to step outside into the light shining down on a porch and sidewalk that weaved through a garden.

Though he'd been to the estate before, Mustang hadn't been there often enough to memorize his way around. Since he'd be staying there indefinitely, he needed to be completely familiar with every building, gate and entry and exit onto the property. He studied what he could in the glow lighting the path.

Once inside the detached garage, Arnold flipped on the light switch.

Mustang blinked. He knew the building was large, but wow. At least twenty cars in a multitude of shapes, models, years and colors formed two rows. "This isn't a garage, it's a warehouse," he muttered.

Arnold nodded. "Mr. Halverson collected cars." He plucked a soft cloth off a shelf and ran it over the hood of a sleek, black Ferrari. "This was one of his favorites."

"Does Charlie drive them?"

"No." Arnold tipped his head toward a long black limousine. "She leaves the drive to the chauffeurs. The traffic in DC is more than she prefers to manage. And many of these wouldn't accommodate her security detail."

"It's a shame no one drives these," Mustang commented. "Why does she keep them?"

"You'll have to ask Mrs. Halverson. I suspect she has a sentimental attachment to them." Arnold folded the soft cloth and replaced it on the shelf. "Your truck is over here." He led the way through a door into another section of the garage where Mustang's black truck was parked next to a four-door sedan Mustang assumed was Grace's. On the other side of the car were three more vehicles he recognized. The black one similar to his belonged to Declan. The charcoal-gray, four-wheel-drive pickup belonged to Mack Balkman, the assistant lead of the team. An olive-drab Hummer was Cole McCastlain's, equipped to transport Dawg, his Belgain Malenoi, his former military war dog. On the far side of the line of vehicles was a Harley-Davidson belonging to Jack Snow. Gus Walsh must have caught a ride with Cole or Mack, otherwise his vehicle would have been in the lineup.

The team had agreed to meet at Charlie's estate before the incident with Emily. Mustang had been on the way when he'd gotten the call. If he hadn't been where he was, Emily would not have survived.

The thought drove him forward to collect his gear. An unexplainable urge to return to the house and lay eyes on his new assignment made him jerk open the truck door and grab the go-bag from behind the rear seat.

"Is that all you need?" Arnold asked.

"That's all." Mustang turned and headed back the way they'd come.

"Pardon me, sir."

Arnold's voice brought Mustang to a halt. He turned, bag in hand, to face the butler.

"Mrs. Halverson asked me to show you an alternate route to return to the main house. She said you never know when it might come in handy. Her words, exactly."

Curious, Mustang returned to Arnold's side. "Lead the way."

The butler spun on his heels and marched toward what appeared to be a wall of tools. When he reached it, he pulled on a shiny wrench. The wall shook slightly and then a door opened outward. Stairs led downward, in the direction of the house.

"They thought of everything," Mustang said.

"Mr. Halverson felt he should always be prepared for any situation."

"What was he expecting, a war?"

Arnold shrugged. "You never know. Now, if you will follow me." The butler descended the stairs. As he reached the bottom, a light blinked on.

When Mustang stepped through, the door behind him closed. He turned to study the mechanism to re-open it should he need to. A lever on the wall beside the door appeared to be how the lock was triggered. Committing it to memory, he hurried after Arnold.

The tunnel was bright white and well-lit. At one point, the pathway split.

Arnold paused long enough to point to the right. "That way leads to the rose arbor at the end of the garden." He didn't go in that direction. Instead he veered left. Soon they were climbing steps up to another door with a similar lever as the one at the garage.

Arnold pulled the lever. As he did, the light in the tunnel snuffed out.

Mustang stopped two steps below Arnold and waited until the door they'd just reached opened inward. Light from above spilled through the gap and flooded the stairwell as the exit grew wider.

They emerged into the study they'd passed on their way through the house. Once Mustang cleared the door, the wall shifted back into place. Wood paneling and a floor-to-ceiling bookcase completely hid the door.

Arnold pointed to a book on one of the

shelves. "If you need to use the tunnel, look for *Moby Dick*."

Mustang leaned forward and read the title on the book binding. *Moby Dick*.

Arnold gave him a slight chin lift. "Go ahead. Give it a try."

Mustang pulled the book, which gave a little resistance. Instead of sliding off the shelf, it tipped and the wall moved, opening to reveal the passage they'd just emerged from.

"I'll take you to your room." Arnold led the way out of the study, up the curving staircase to the second floor of the three-story mansion and turned right. He walked down a long hallway and stopped at a door. "You'll be in this room." The butler nodded at one door farther down the hallway. "Miss Chastain is in the room beside you. There is a connecting door should you need to use it." He pushed open the hall door and stood back for Mustang to enter. "When you've deposited your gear, Mrs. Halverson would like the team to meet in the conference room."

"Roger," Mustang responded automatically. His lips twisted. "You weren't perhaps in the military at some time, were you?"

Arnold gave a slight nod and met Mustang's gaze. "Ten years in the SAS."

Mustang held out his hand. "Always good to meet a brother in arms."

Arnold shook the man's hand. "Always good to have help you can count on." With a nod, he left Mustang and marched down the hallway.

For a long moment Mustang watched the former SAS operative. Only then did he notice a slight limp. Despite Arnold's limp, Mustang bet the butler could hold his own in a fight. Mrs. Halverson was lucky to have him on staff. Though, to Mustang, being a butler was only a small portion of Arnold's duties. He was her first line of defense in the mansion.

Mustang dropped his gear on the bed and unzipped the bag. It had been several weeks since he'd packed the duffel. He removed the items quickly, throwing clothes in a drawer and his ammo on top of the dresser. When the bag was empty, he zipped it and stored it in the closet. Then he walked to the door connecting to the other room and pressed his ear to the panel. He could hear the sound of a shower and twisted the knob to see if it was locked.

The knob turned easily.

Rather than barge in, he released the knob and left the door closed. He would have liked to see Emily before going downstairs, but he couldn't wait. His team was waiting for him in the conference room. He strode to the French doors, stepped out onto the balcony and leaned over to check the window of the room beside him. No trees grew close enough for someone to climb and gain entry. No ladders had been left nearby and the brick and rock walls were clear of any trellises or climbing vines.

Relatively certain Emily would be all right in the house, Mustang made his way back down the stairs, past a living room and into the study. A door led from inside the study, down a hidden staircase into the basement and a soundproof space Mr. Halverson had used as a conference room before his untimely death. A fourteen-foot mahogany conference table took up much of the room with enough chairs to seat a dozen people. The side walls contained magnetic Dry-Erase whiteboards. Several computer terminals were positioned along the walls with six monitors each, arranged in an array.

Cole McCastlain, the team's radio operator and all-around computer guru, sat at one of the keyboards, alternating between typing furiously and clicking on the mouse.

Gus Walsh and Jack Snow stood behind him, peering over his shoulder at the information on the center screen. While they worked, they ate. A sideboard was set up buffet-style with sandwiches, salads, drinks and something warm and delicious-smelling that Emily guessed was lasagna. When Grace saw her eyeing it, she quickly fixed Emily and Mustang plates and set them on the table.

"For when you're hungry," she said to them both.

"What have you learned about Emily's attacker?" Mustang asked.

"Nothing, yet," Jack said. "We're not even sure where to start."

Declan, Mack, Grace and Charlie stood before another set of monitors set up with several news channel displays, the volume on each turned down low but loud enough they could hear.

Grace stared at one of the television monitors, her brows furrowed. "Emily was at the Russian embassy today. She said she was translating for the ambassador, but couldn't divulge what was said."

Charlie shifted her gaze from one news station to another. "I thought I heard something about an altercation at the Russian embassy earlier today. They had a lockdown. Surely they'll say something about it on the evening news."

"The lockdown must have happened after Emily left," Declan noted.

"I have contacts at a couple of the news stations and local newspapers," Charlie said. "I could call around and get the scoop."

"Wait." Grace pointed to a screen. "Turn that one up."

Mack grabbed the remote and adjusted the volume louder.

A reporter stood in front of large building in downtown DC. Behind him were at least a dozen police cars, SWAT vehicles and fire trucks. He glanced behind him and back at the camera. "Today, at approximately three forty-five in the afternoon, the Russian embassy locked its gates and refused to let anyone in or out. So far, no one inside is talking to explain why they've instituted a lockdown. The State Department has reached out to Russia for answers, but so far no one knows why the Russian embassy has been shut down or who might still be inside."

"What are they saying?" a voice said from behind Mustang. "The Russian embassy is in lockdown?"

Mustang turned to face Emily. Her long blond hair lay in damp strands around her shoulders and her face was scrubbed clean of any makeup. The clothes she wore hung loose on her frame, just some sweatpants and a T-shirt, and she stood barefooted on the Persian rug.

Grace went to her friend, slipped an arm around her shoulders and led her toward the television monitors. "They had a lockdown around three forty-five this afternoon."

"That was right after I left." Emily shook her head. "What happened?"

"No one knows," Charlie said. "No one is getting in or out of the embassy at this time."

"And no one is talking," Declan added. "Did you see or hear anything on your way in or out?"

Emily shook her head. "No."

"Can you share what you translated while inside the embassy?" Mack asked.

Again Emily shook her head, shifting from one foot to the other, her discomfort apparent. "I signed nondisclosure statements. But I can tell you, it was more of a personal nature than political. I wouldn't think it would cause a lockdown."

"Well, something did," Charlie said. "And I wonder who is still inside and why."

Emily looked back at the monitors. "Did they say anything about a Mr. Phillips? He was the man whose report I translated. He was still there when I left the embassy."

Grace responded. "No, nothing."

Mustang stepped up beside Emily and

cupped her elbow. He leaned close and whispered, "Are you all right?"

She glanced up into his eyes, a small, grateful smile curling her lips. She gave him a silent nod and leaned into his arm. Together they faced the wall of monitors.

Several of the newscasts displayed various reporters standing in front of the Russian embassy, all reporting on the lockdown. As if on cue, they cut to commercials, all except one station that flashed a still image of a young man on the screen. The man held a microphone, a strand of his dark hair falling over his forehead like an unintentional fashion statement.

Emily gave a small gasp and stiffened against Mustang.

He stared down at her. "What's wrong?"

"I saw that man."

"Where?" Grace asked.

"At the embassy before I left," Emily said. Her brow furrowed. "What are they saying about him?"

"Turn it up," Mustang commanded.

Mack adjusted the volume.

The picture was replaced by a female news anchor. "So far, we have received no word from Tyler Blunt. He was supposed to report in yesterday evening with the station manager, but he hasn't. He hasn't been to his apartment in two days and he isn't answering his phone. If anyone has any information about Tyler Blunt's whereabouts, please notify this station."

"He was in the embassy," Emily said.

"Are you sure?"

Emily nodded. "He was on his way in as I was on my way out."

"Was he going willingly?" Mustang asked.

Emily frowned. "I wasn't sure. They were hustling me out at that time. The young man was flanked by a couple of men."

Grace gripped her arms. "Emily, a reporter is missing. One you saw at the Russian embassy. Then you were attacked after leaving the embassy. Doesn't that sound too coincidental?"

Mustang's jaw tightened. "I don't believe in coincidence."

Emily looked over Grace's shoulder into Mustang's eyes, her own widening. "Neither do I. But what do I have to do with the reporter?"

Chapter Five

Mustang shook his head. "Maybe your attack and Tyler Blunt's disappearance have nothing to do with each other. But my gut is telling me otherwise."

A chill rippled down the back of Emily's neck. "I've never even met Tyler Blunt. Sure, I've seen him on television news reports, but I've never actually had words with him. Why would he and I have anything in common? Other than being in the Russian embassy at the same time, we've never been anywhere closer. There has to be another reason for the attack on me."

Charlie's eyes narrowed. "Well, we won't know unless we start asking questions." She glanced across the room at Declan.

Declan nodded. "We're on it." He nodded toward Gus who had been busy clicking away on the mouse and the keyboard of the computer he'd been working for as long as Emily had been in the conference room. "We have Gus searching for anything that might raise red flags."

Mustang's eyes narrowed. "Cross-check anything related to the Russian ambassador and Tyler Blunt."

"Already have," Cole confirmed. "Nothing is coming up tying Blunt with the ambassador, Nikolai Kozlov. But I'm not finished digging. It could take some time."

"We might have to get out on the street and ask questions," Mustang said.

"In the meantime, I still have a job to do," Emily said. "I'm supposed to teach a class in Russian literature tomorrow."

"Can't you call in sick?" Charlie asked.

She shook her head. "No. We have a major test coming up. I'm going over everything we've covered for the first half of the semester. Then I'm adminstering the test. I have to be there."

"Once you step foot off Charlie's estate, you could become a target all over again." Mustang said. "Could you pass your notes to someone else and let them perform the review?"

Emily crossed her arms over her chest. "I can't bail on my students."

Mustang frowned heavily. "Their grades mean more to you than your life?"

"They've all worked hard," she said. "If it were any other day in the semester, I might consider skipping. But it's the only class day they have left before midterms. I owe it to them to be there."

"And how will they respond to having a stranger in their classroom?" Mustang stood taller, his shoulders back, his chin held high.

Emily studied the man. Her reaction was probably not a good indication of how the other young men and women would react to the big marine standing or sitting among them. He was far too handsome and built like a tank. Every red-blooded cell in her veins stood up and applauded at the determined man, standing with his shoulders back and head held high.

Her heart pounded and her voice came out as a squeak. "They'll…" She cleared her throat and started again. "They'll have to deal with it, I suppose." Emily pushed her shoulders back and stood as tall as her five feet, four inches could manage against Mustang's much larger stance. "I have to be there."

Mustang's lips twitched. "So be it. We'll be there." He turned to Declan. "And then we'll come right back here."

Before he finished the last word, she was shaking her head. "I want to go by my apartment and gather some of my clothing and toiletries." She shot a glance at Grace. "No offense, but I like wearing my own things."

Grace smiled. "None taken. I prefer my own stuff, myself."

Mustang nodded. "Okay, but then we're heading right back to this estate."

Again Emily shook her head. "While we're out, I'd like to stop by the office of the organization that hired me as an interpreter. Maybe they will know something about what happened today."

"I know you signed a nondisclosure agreement," Mustang said. "But can you tell us who was involved in the meeting where you translated Russian?"

Emily chewed on her bottom lip. She was not at liberty to tell them what was said, but nowhere in that agreement had it stipulated she couldn't talk about who else was involved. "I was interpreting for an American private investigator. Jay Phillips."

"We'll look him up," Declan said. "And it wouldn't hurt to pay him a visit."

Emily frowned. "My nondisclosure didn't specifically say I couldn't talk about who was in the meeting. But telling you the investigator's name might be construed as crossing the line."

Declan nodded. "Fair enough. We'll tread

lightly when we confront him. Mostly, we want to find out if he's suffering some of the same problems as you are. And if so, we might conclude that whatever was discussed at the meeting could have something to do with whoever is trying to kill you."

Declan's Defenders dug into the buffet, while they went over and over the events leading up to Emily being run off the road. They considered every detail, every angle, as they ate. By the time they finished, Emily was certain she'd have nightmares for the rest of her life.

After everyone had eaten, Emily helped carry plates to the massive kitchen, eager to escape the inquisition. She placed her dishes on the counter beside the sink. When she turned, she almost ran into Mustang.

"Sorry," she said. "I didn't know you were there."

"It's okay," he said. "I was following too close."

Standing so near to Mustang caused a ripple of awareness to shoot across her skin and make her shiver. Emily spun back to the sink, put the stopper in the drain, and started filling it with water and soap.

"My staff will take care of the cleanup," Charlie said.

"If it's all the same to you, Charlie," Emily

said, "I need something to keep myself busy. So much has happened that if I don't have anything to do, I'll just dwell on the bad."

Charlie brought her plate to the sink, laid it on the counter and then pressed a hand to Emily's arm. "I understand. I need to keep busy, as well. When my husband died, I went through the entire house cleaning."

"But you have a staff to do all that," Emily pointed out.

Charlie snorted. "Tell me about it. I confused the hell out of them." She chuckled softly. "And you know how big this house is."

Emily glanced her way. "That must have taken you days."

"I called it vacuum therapy. I made a lot of noise with the vacuum, so I could yell when I was mad and nobody would care or hear me. And when I was done, I had a clean house. The added bonus was that I was worn out and finally able to sleep." She waved at the sink. "So have at it."

"Thank you," Emily said.

Charlie smiled and left the kitchen.

Emily slipped her hands into the warm, soapy water as if reaching for some level of normalcy.

Mustang moved up beside her and handed her a plate. "You wash, I'll dry."

"I can do this by myself," she said, not at all certain she wanted the added complication of standing next to a man who made her body hum.

"I know you can do this by yourself," he said. "That was a lot of excitement for one day. I can use the work, as well."

Emily settled into washing each dish carefully before handing it to Mustang to rinse and dry. She felt a sense of safety and comfort with the big marine standing beside her. But every time her hand touched his, a shock of electricity slipped up her arm and spread warmth across her chest. What was it about the man that made her so aware of him? Other than the fact that he stood a head taller than her, and his shoulders were as broad as a door frame. Something about his rugged countenance and his take-charge attitude sent shivers across her skin.

Grace entered the kitchen carrying a stack of plates. "Need help in here?"

Emily almost said yes. Not that she needed help washing dishes. What she needed was help understanding what was going on inside her head and body. Before she could open her mouth to tell Grace yes, she needed help, Mustang answered for her.

"No, thank you, we've got this covered," he said.

"Okay then," Grace said. "If you get a chance, check out the garden. Charlie has the most wonderful roses and a fountain that can be very soothing to sit in front of. And at night everything smells divine."

"I'll do that," Emily promised.

Once all the dishes were deposited in the kitchen, the rest of the team retired to the living area, leaving Mustang and Emily alone to wash.

For a long time they worked in silence, washing and drying one plate, one glass, one fork at a time. Finally, feeling a little out of breath and rattled, Emily handed the last dish to Mustang. While he dried, she wiped her hands on a towel and hung the towel to dry. Despite the mind-numbing work of washing dishes, she still felt nervous and punchy. Perhaps it was from having been shot at, or maybe it was the big marine who had been standing next to her bumping shoulders with her for the last thirty minutes. But Emily had to move, had to leave the room. Needed to get out, needed some fresh air.

"Thank you for helping by drying." She turned and started for the door leading out of the kitchen.

"Hey, wait," Mustang called out.

Emily turned.

Mustang quickly dried the last dish and put it in the cabinet along with the rest. He laid the towel across the oven rail and rubbed his hands along the sides of his jeans. "I'll go with you."

"That's not necessary," Emily said. "I'm just going to wander around the house. I shouldn't run into any problems inside the Halverson estate."

Mustang's brow dipped. "Well, I guess that's okay. But if you decide to go outside for any reason, let me know and I'll go with you."

"Deal." Emily turned and walked away. She wanted to put distance between her and the marine. Following the sound of voices, she entered the living area where the others had congregated.

Grace glanced up from where she was perched on the arm of a sofa next to Declan and smiled. "Thank you for doing dishes."

Emily nodded. "No problem. It helped me work through some of my nerves."

Grace chuckled. "I can think of much better ways to burn off some steam. But whatever works for you, I'm glad it did."

Declan waved toward the other end of the sofa. "Won't you join us?"

Emily shook her head. "Thank you, no. I

don't feel much like sitting." She glanced at Charlie. "If you don't mind, I'd like to explore the house."

Charlie smiled. "Go right ahead. Make yourself at home."

"Do you need someone to show you around?" Grace asked.

Emily gave her half a smile. "No, thank you. I'd like to do it on my own. I need some time to think."

Emily left the living room and walked to the next door down the hallway and entered. Inside this room were some more feminine-looking sofas and a white baby grand piano. Drawn to the musical instrument, she entered the room, crossed to the piano and ran her fingers across the keys.

The cool, white ivories against her fingertips brought back memories she thought she'd forgotten. She hadn't touched a piano since she'd left home almost a decade before. Emily couldn't remember a time as a child when she hadn't been taking piano lessons or going to recitals. Her parents had made absolutely sure that she, as their only child, would have some musical skills as well as learning a foreign language.

Teaching Russian at the university seemed so natural. Her musical skills were adequate but not sufficient to take to the stage. Quietly, so as not to draw attention away from the conversations in the other room, she played one of her favorite tunes that she had committed to memory.

Even after ten years her fingers found the keys. The music was a liltingly sad tune that suited her mood. Soon she was lost in time and the sound of the keys hitting against the chords. When the song came to an end she lifted her fingers from the keys and sat for a moment staring at the instrument.

Until she had sat at Charlie's piano, she hadn't realized just how much she missed playing. And how cathartic the music was to her soul.

"That was beautiful."

Jerked back to the present, Emily shot a glance to the door where Mustang leaned against the doorjamb, a gentle smile tugging at the corners of his lips.

"How long have you been standing there?" she asked, heat rising up her neck.

Mustang straightened and walked toward her. "Since you sat down and started playing." He closed the distance and leaned against the grand piano. "I didn't have the heart to interrupt. In fact, I didn't want to interrupt. I didn't want you to know I was there because you looked so at peace and so engrossed in what you were doing. And, call me selfish, but I liked listening. I didn't want you to stop."

Warmth burned up into her cheeks. Emily glanced down at her fingers on the piano keys. "I haven't played in ten years. It must have sounded awful."

Mustang chuckled.

The deep, resonant sound made her shiver all over.

"If that was awful, then I am tone deaf." His smile disappeared. "Don't stop on my account. If you want, I'll leave the room."

Emily shook her head, pushed back from the piano and stood. "No, really, I'm done," she said. "I haven't made it very far in my exploration of the estate."

Mustang's smile returned. "Uh, right. One room over is not very far. Not when you consider the size of this estate. I believe it's over twelve thousand square feet, just the house alone, and the garage is like a warehouse. There must be over twenty thousand square feet just in the garage alone."

Emily walked around him, giving him plenty of space. She didn't want to touch him for fear of having that electrical shock shoot through her again. "Sounds like you've already done your exploring. You must visit here quite a lot."

"It's our base of operations." Mustang fell into step behind her.

She had hoped he wouldn't follow her. But when the sound of his footsteps continued on her heels, she stopped suddenly.

He bumped into her.

"Look." She spun on her heels to find herself standing toe to toe with Mustang. "Could I have a little space? I don't need you following me around inside the house."

Mustang held up his hands. "Sorry, I didn't mean to crowd you."

Emily raised her hands. They fluttered a little, so close to his chest she could touch him. And that was the problem. She sighed. "I just need some time to myself, to think. To breathe. To get a grasp on what happened today."

Mustang captured her flapping hands in his big, warm paws. "I get it. I'll let you be alone."

She should have pulled her hands free, but the warmth of his fingers holding hers made her want to continue just like that until her heartbeat stopped fluttering so fast.

Instead of slowing to a calm, steady beat, her pulse raced even faster. "I have to go." She pulled her hands free, turned and ran. When she reached the hallway, she looked in both directions. Though alone, she wasn't sure where she should go next.

When she saw the study across the hall, she darted into the room lined with bookshelves. Emily loved books. They were her escape, her wells of knowledge, and her friends when she wanted to be alone but not completely alone.

The ornate wood paneling of the study lined the walls and ceiling. A massive mahogany desk took up one end of the room. To the side was a set of wood-framed French doors.

With her need to escape driving her forward, Emily aimed for the French doors, charging across the room, pulling the handle and stepping out into the night.

Cool night air felt good against her flushed cheeks as she turned to quietly close the French doors behind her. The soft glow of accent lights guided her along a path leading toward a garden. She guessed it was the rose garden Grace had talked about. She could smell them before she even reached the space. The aroma filled her, wrapped around her and soothed her scattered senses.

Neatly trimmed rosebushes lined the walkway with fragrant blooms in a multitude of colors. In the center of the garden stood a fountain. Water bubbled from the top, dropping down to the lower levels. Stone benches surrounded the fountain, inviting Emily to sit. She dropped onto the smooth, stone surface and rested her face in her hands. So much had happened in the last twelve hours that she could barely wrap her mind around everything.

Her day had started with her Advanced Russian Language class. She'd gone straight from there to the Russian embassy where she had interpreted for the investigator and the ambassador.

Emily snorted. And she'd thought the Russian ambassador had troubles with his daughter having an affair with an American. He only had to deal with a rebellious daughter. Emily had had to deal with somebody shooting at her or trying to run her over or off the road.

Why did someone want her dead?

She glanced up at the fountain as if it could give her the answers. But the trickling water just continued to dribble, drip and soothe. But not enough. What she needed was answers. The fountain couldn't give them to her, and the roses were no help, other than to smell pretty. She needed to get out and to ask the questions that would lead her to the answers. Hiding away on Charlie's estate would get her nowhere.

Emily squared her shoulders and started to rise. The snap of a twig made her start. She rose and paused, listening. Was that the shuffle of footsteps? Had Mustang followed her out to the garden?

"Mustang?" she called out softly and then listened, straining her ears to hear anything. Her pulse pounded so loudly against her eardrums she could barely discern the sound of the wind rustling in the leaves.

Mustang had asked her to let him know when she went outside. He'd had a reason for that. Even though the estate was equipped with security cameras and guards, someone could possibly get past them.

Someone who wanted to kill her.

Emily started toward the path leading back to the study and the French doors she had come through. She tiptoed softly, listening as she went, creeping along slowly. With the ever-increasing beat of her heart, she moved faster until she was running.

She burst through the French doors and crashed into a wall of muscle.

Chapter Six

"Hey," a deep voice said. Arms wrapped around her and held her close. "I thought I told you to let me know when you went outside."

She buried her face against his chest. "You did. I didn't. I wish I had."

He stiffened, his arms enfolding her tightly. "What's wrong?"

Emily felt foolish. But she didn't want to push away from his warm embrace. "I don't know. I probably was hearing things."

"You want to stay here while I check it out?"

"No," she said and enveloped her arms around his waist, pressing her face closer to his chest.

"You wanna come with me?" he asked.

"No. Can't we just stay here?" she said, her voice muffled against his shirt.

"We can do that, too." He pulled her closer and rested his chin against the top of her head. "We can stay here as long as you like."

"Good," she said. Her lips pushed against his shirt.

"I don't mind holding you like this, but could we at least get away from the windows?" Mustang whispered.

She nodded.

He guided both of them away from the windows and deeper into the study.

Emily didn't know how long she stood there until her heartbeat slowed to a more normal pace, but it didn't seem nearly long enough.

Mustang didn't say another word, just held her.

When at last she raised her head, she gave him a crooked grin. "I'm sorry."

"What's there to be sorry for?" Mustang touched a finger to the side of her cheek. "You had quite the scare today." He pressed his lips to her forehead and then leaned back. "You okay now?"

She nodded, although her pulse had ratcheted up with the feel of his lips against her forehead.

Mustang shifted one of his hands from around her waist to cup the back of her head. "So, what was it you heard outside?"

She gave a broken laugh. "It was probably a stick falling from the tree. The wind was blowing a little. I'm sure it was nothing."

Mustang cupped her cheek. "Still, I'd like to check it out."

Voices sounded in the hallway.

"Oh, there you are." Declan entered the room, followed by Grace.

Emily stepped away from Mustang. Heat rushed into her cheeks.

"We're trying to contact the private investigator that Emily had interpreted for," Declan said, as if continuing a conversation.

"You think he might have had something to do with this?" Mustang asked.

Declan shook his head. "No, but if Emily is having difficulties, he might also have run into some problems. We tried looking him up and phoning but got no answer. We don't have his cell info, though. Not yet. We'll find his place and head there tomorrow if we still can't raise a response by then."

Grace crossed to get close to Emily and hooked her arm through Emily's. "Are you doing okay?"

"I'm fine."

Grace frowned. "You look a little flushed. Are you sure you're not feverish?"

Emily shook her head. "No, I was just outside for a few minutes."

Grace smiled. "Did you get to visit the rose garden?"

Emily nodded. "It was as you said...beautiful."

"The roses seem to be even more vibrant as the weather cools," Grace said.

Emily nodded again. She'd been too frightened by the sounds of the night to care.

Mustang tipped his head toward the door. "While Emily was out in the garden a few minutes ago, she thought she heard something."

Declan's eyes widened. "You think someone was out there?"

Mustang shrugged. "I don't know. But I'd feel better if someone checked it out."

Declan nodded. "Will do. I'll get Snow to go look with me."

"Good," Mustang said. "I'll stay with Emily."

Declan left the study, calling out in the hallway, "Snow. Got a mission for you."

Grace frowned and stared into Emily's eyes. "What did you hear in the garden?"

"I don't know. Could just be my imagination playing tricks on me."

Grace shook her head. "The guys will make sure. With all the stress, you must be exhausted."

It wasn't until Grace mentioned it that Emily realized she had been tense. Her muscles were tired, and she was starting to feel all the aches and pains of having fallen in the dirt and from being tackled from behind. Her knees still stung and her shoulder felt bruised. "I am tired."

Grace slipped an arm around her waist. "I can give you a tour of the estate tomorrow. Why don't you hit the hay and get some much-needed rest?"

Emily's gaze slid to Mustang's.

He nodded. "Go on. I'll be up in a few minutes. My room is next to yours. If you have any troubles in the night, you just have to call out and I'll be right there."

Though she hated being dependent on anyone, Emily was grateful that Mustang was there and would be on the other side of the door to her bedroom.

She let Grace guide her to the staircase and up to her room. Her friend entered with her and nodded at the French doors on the opposite end of the room. "I love that this room has its own balcony and bathroom."

"It's nice," Emily muttered. Perhaps after a good night's sleep, she might be more enthusiastic, but right now she was too tired to care.

Grace lifted a garment from the end of the queen-size bed. "I found an extra nightgown that you can use until we can get to your apartment and get some of your own things." She laid it back on the comforter and turned to face her. "I wish I had more, but we only just moved a few of our things into our rooms."

"Thank you," Emily said. "I hate to be a bother."

"You're not a bother. What are friends for?" Grace hugged her tightly, then let go and stepped away. "If you need anything tonight, all you have to do is ask."

Tears welled in Emily's eyes. "You've been so good to me."

Grace left her in her room, softly closing the door behind her.

For a long moment Emily stood staring at the nightgown on the bed. Her gaze shifted to the door connecting her room to the one Mustang would be sleeping in that night. A shiver of awareness rippled across her skin. She wasn't quite sure what she was afraid of most. Her attacker...or her lusty attraction to the big marine who had saved her life that day.

MUSTANG MET UP with his team in the hallway as they headed for the door leading out the back of the estate. "What's the plan?" he asked.

Declan nodded at the others. "We're going to check out the garden and do a reconnaissance of the perimeter to make sure everything is in place and the security system is working."

Mustang clapped his hands together, ready

to dive into the mission. "Which way do you want me to go?"

"Go with Arnold," Declan said. "He's going to check the front gate."

"Will do." Mustang performed an about-face and headed toward the front of the house where he joined Arnold.

The butler unbuttoned his suit jacket and pulled it to the side, displaying a shoulder holster and handgun tucked inside.

Mustang nodded and pulled his jacket aside to display his own shoulder holster and handgun beneath. No words were necessary for each to know the other was armed.

Arnold opened the front door and they both stepped outside. Rather than walking down the road winding toward the gate, they slipped into the shadows and worked their way quickly, paralleling the road all the way to the front of the estate near the entrance. When they arrived at the gate, Mustang held back in the shadows, providing cover for Arnold as he checked mechanisms to ensure they were working properly. Once his task was complete, he slipped back into the shadows and joined Mustang where he stood.

"Everything seems to be functioning as intended," said the butler.

A soft whistle sounded in the darkness.

Arnold reached for the handgun beneath his jacket.

Mustang touched his arm. "That's one of my guys, indicating he's nearby. That way we don't shoot first and ask questions later."

"Good to know," Arnold acknowledged.

The whistle was one they had used during operations in Afghanistan. A moment later Snow emerged from the shadows and joined them.

"Anything?" Mustang asked.

Snow shook his head. "Not a thing."

Arnold tipped his head toward the stone wall with its wrought-iron gate. "Gate's secure."

"Meet back at the conference room?" Snow asked.

"I'm gonna check the property line on the other side of the gate." Mustang turned and started along the fence line.

"I'll come with you," Snow offered.

They hadn't gone two steps when the sound of an engine revving cut through the night. In the next moment, a loud crash sounded behind them.

Mustang and Snow spun.

A commercial-size dump truck had crashed through the stone wall, leaving it in rubble.

Mustang pulled his handgun from beneath

his jacket and aimed it at the truck's driver's-side cab.

Snow did the same.

"Arnold?" Mustang called out.

"I'm okay," he called from the other side of the crashed vehicle.

The truck engine was no longer running, but steam poured out from the radiator beneath the hood.

Clinging to the shadows, Mustang and Snow eased up on the driver's side of the vehicle. From what Mustang could see, there was no one in the driver's seat, or he was lying down.

"I don't see anybody inside," Mustang said.

"That doesn't mean there isn't anyone in there." Snow eased up to the door. "You cover. I'll open."

Mustang took a position where he could fire straight into the cab once the door was open.

Ducking low, Snow reached for the handle on the pickup and threw open the door.

Mustang aimed, his finger barely caressing the trigger and held his fire. As far as he could tell in the darkness, there was no one in the truck. "Clear," he confirmed.

"Clear on this side," Arnold echoed.

Mustang crawled over the rubble to the back of the truck. He didn't find anyone there, either.

"Check this out," Snow said.

Mustang scrambled back over the bits of stone to the cab of the pickup where Snow had leaned in, studying the interior. His teammate backed out and waved for Mustang to lean in.

"He rigged the accelerator by strapping a heavy brick to it." Snow snorted. "But why?"

Mustang's gaze met Snow's and a cold chill ripped across his spine. "Diversionary tactic."

They turned as one toward the house and ran. Declan, Gus, Mack and Cole joined them before they reached the house and fell in beside them as they raced.

"What the hell was that?" Declan asked.

"I'll explain when we get to the house," Mustang yelled. He kept running, his heart thundering against his ribs. He prayed he wasn't too late.

Chapter Seven

Emily had just slipped into the nightgown and robe Grace had provided when she heard the crashing sound. She ran to the French doors, flung them open and stepped out onto the balcony. A cool breeze ruffled the hem of her nightgown and chilled her arms and legs. Behind her, she heard her bedroom door open and close. Still straining to see what had caused the commotion, Emily assumed it was Grace.

"What was that?" she asked without turning.

Footsteps sounded, coming quickly. Before she was aware of the danger, she was shoved from behind.

Emily slammed into the balcony railing and doubled over, pitching over the edge. She flailed, reaching out, trying to find purchase. Her fingers wrapped around the wrought-iron rail and hung on tightly as her body weight jerked her grip loose. Emily screamed. Again the door to her bedroom opened.

"Emily!" Grace yelled.

A man all dressed in black with a black ski mask pulled over his face stood over her.

"Help me!" Emily called out, her arm aching and fingers slipping loose.

A shot rang out.

The man in black vaulted over the railing, grabbing her legs as he came down.

The added weight made her fingers slip free of their grip and she dropped from the second-story balcony, landing with a thud on top of the intruder who'd dragged her down. Not only had he ended up breaking her fall; he'd had the wind knocked out of him and lay still for blessed moments. Now was her chance.

Emily took the opportunity to scramble to her feet and dart away. And she almost made it, but a hand grabbed a hold of her ankle and yanked her back.

"Emily," Grace cried from above. "If you can get away, move to the side so I can get a clean shot."

"Emily! Grace!" cried out male voices in the darkness.

The man holding her ankle released it and scrambled to his feet.

Another shot rang out, the sound reverberating in the darkness.

Her masked attacker stumbled but kept running. As he disappeared into the darkness, the men of Declan's Defenders appeared from the opposite direction.

Emily pointed. "That way!"

Five of the six men took off running after the disappearing attacker.

Mustang stayed behind. Instead of following his counterparts, he hooked an arm around her shoulders and hustled her toward the back door leading into the house.

As soon as they reached the door, Emily turned and braced her hands against Mustang's chest. "Don't worry about me. Go get him," she said.

Mustang shook his head. "I'm not going anywhere." He edged her in through the door and closed it behind them. Then his gaze raked her from head to toe. "Are you okay?"

As the adrenaline rush receded, Emily could feel every one of the bumps and bruises she had acquired in her fall. "I—think I'm okay."

"What were you doing outside?" he asked. "I thought you'd gone to bed?"

"I heard a crash," she said. "I went out onto my balcony to see what had happened."

"Then how did you end up down here?"

She snorted. "The attacker hit me from inside my bedroom and knocked me over the railing."

Mustang's eyes widened. "You fell from the

balcony?" His gaze scanned her once again, slower this time as he seemed to make sure she really was in one piece. "Sweet heaven, you could have broken your neck.

Emily nodded.

Mustang shook his head. "We need to get you to a hospital and check you out for a concussion."

"No need," she said. "I didn't hit my head. In fact, I landed on my attacker."

The next thing she knew, Emily was being scooped up into Mustang's arms and carried into the living room. Nestled against his chest, Emily had to admit she felt safer there. But at the same time, unsettled and very aware of the man.

"I'm quite all right. I can walk on my own," she insisted.

He didn't answer, just kept walking.

"Seriously, I can walk." Emily didn't struggle. She told herself it was because she didn't want to throw him off balance. But the truth was, she really didn't want him to put her down. And he didn't put her down until they reached the living room and he laid her on the couch.

"I'm calling the doctor." He reached for the telephone.

"Don't." Emily shot up from the couch and

put her hand over his. That same electric jolt shot through her arm and into her chest that had startled her earlier when they'd first touched. For a moment she forgot what she was going to say. Then it came back to her. "I tell you, I'm okay." She held her arms out to the sides and smiled. "See?"

Mustang frowned mightily. "I'd feel better if you had a doctor at least check to see if you have any concussion."

Emily chuckled softly. "I didn't hit my head. If anybody hit their head, it was my attacker. He's the one who needs to see a doctor about a concussion."

"Hopefully they'll catch him so that they can give him a concussion or send him to the hospital." Mustang ran a hand through his hair.

Emily rubbed her arms with her hands, suddenly aware she was wearing only her night clothes. "I hope they catch him, too."

Mustang stared at her for a moment. Then he reached out and pulled her into his embrace. "Are you cold?"

Emily shrugged. "Not really. I think it's just that the adrenaline has run its course." She shivered, her entire body quaking.

Mustang closed his arms around her, pulled her really close and rested his chin on top of her head. "You scared the crap out of me."

She laughed. "Scared the crap out of *you*? That man scared the crud out of me. I don't ever want to fall off a balcony again."

"I don't ever want you to fall off a balcony again." For a long moment he held her without saying a word.

Emily didn't move. She enjoyed being up against him with the strength of his muscles beneath her fingertips.

They remained that way until footsteps sounded in the hallway.

"Oh, Emily. Thank God." Grace entered the room and rushed toward her.

Emily stepped back from Mustang to be engulfed in Grace's embrace.

"I nearly had a heart attack. When you went over the balcony rail, I thought for sure you were dead." She hugged Emily so tightly she could barely breathe.

Emily leaned back. "Was it my imagination or were you firing at my attacker?"

Grace grinned. "Don't worry, I've had a lot of practice. I'm a pretty good shot."

"As long as I'm not the one you're shooting at." Emily shook her head, a smile tilting her lips. "When did you learn to fire a gun?"

"Declan's been taking me to the range. He even bought me an HK .40-caliber pistol and a shoulder holster." She patted her jacket and opened it, showing the pistol tucked beneath her arm. "It took some time getting used to wearing it. But I'm glad I did."

Emily laughed. "You and me both." She shivered and rubbed her hands up and down her arms.

Mustang slipped out of his jacket and draped it over Emily's shoulders.

She smiled up at him, grateful for the gesture. The leather jacket still radiated Mustang's body heat and smelled of his cologne. Emily could easily get lost in how good it felt.

Declan, Gus and Jack Snow entered the room.

Mustang's gaze shot to them. "Did you catch him?"

Declan shook his head. "Snow is our fastest runner. He made it out to the fence in time to see the man climb a ladder over the top."

"Why didn't he get him while he was on the ladder?" Mustang asked.

"He was at the top of the fence before Snow could get to him, and then he pushed the ladder to the ground," Declan said.

"He had a car waiting on the other side," Gus said. "By the time Snow got the ladder back up and was at the top of the fence, the guy got away in his car."

"Did you get a license plate?" Mustang asked. He knew the answer before Gus responded.

Gus shook his head. "No license plates."

"I wish we knew why he was targeting Emily." Mustang paced the floor.

Charlie entered the room. "I put a call out for the police. They should be here in the next five minutes."

"I don't know what good they'll be," Emily said. "The guy was wearing gloves. He would not have left any fingerprints."

"Then he wouldn't have left fingerprints in the truck he used to smash the fence," Mustang said.

"And he had to have had some help. He probably had someone waiting in the car to drive him away," Gus said.

"That's right, there have been two men working the operation," Declan said. "One to provide the diversion. The other to get inside the fence."

Mustang stopped pacing, coming to a halt in front of Emily. "All I know is that Emily isn't even safe inside the perimeter of the Halverson estate."

Declan nodded. "Agreed. That's why I've got Mack and Cole guarding the perimeter." Declan tipped his chin toward Mustang. "I need you to stay with Emily through the night. We can't count on her being safe even inside the house. As we've already seen."

Mustang locked gazes with Emily. "She's not getting out of my sight."

Emily's body quivered.

"You two need to get some rest," Declan said. "Tomorrow you're going to the Russian language training class with Emily."

Mustang nodded. "I guess I'd better bone up on my Russian."

Emily tilted her head to the side. "You speak Russian?"

"A little," Mustang said. "It's not like I have a chance to use it much."

Emily grinned. "Then you can help me grade papers."

"Uh, no. My Russian isn't that good."

Declan chuckled. "You haven't heard his Russian."

Mustang's lips twitched. "My Russian is about at the kindergarten level."

"That would be better than most people's," Emily said.

"Tomorrow, Mack and I will chase down the private investigator." He glanced at Emily. "Is there any chance that we can talk to some of the staff at the embassy?"

Emily shrugged. "Some of them live at the embassy. But for the most part they live on the economy. They have apartments and houses just like the rest of us."

"Then I'll see what Cole can find on the computer. Perhaps we can dig up some addresses and go and question some of the staff to see what might be going on with them."

"Don't forget, I'd like to make a stop at my apartment tomorrow and gather some of my things. I can't continue to borrow from Grace," Emily said.

Mustang nodded. "We can do that."

The police arrived and Arnold ushered them into the living room. They all gave statements on what they'd seen and what had happened to Emily that day. The police made a cursory investigation of Emily's bedroom. As Emily had suspected, they found no fingerprints.

Emily and the others waited in the living room until the police finished their search and left.

By that time, it was getting late and Emily was beyond tired. She glanced down at the robe and nightgown Grace had loaned her and the dirt smeared across them. "I guess I'm going for another shower," she said. She glanced up at Mustang. "I guess you'll have to take your eyes off of me long enough to let me have some privacy in the bathroom."

"Are there any windows in the bathroom?" Mustang asked.

"No," Emily said.

"As long as you let me clear the bathroom first, I'll allow you that privacy."

She raised her eyebrows. "Allow?"

Mustang gave her a twisted grin. "Until we get this attacker situation resolved, you'll have to play by my rules."

Emily frowned. "I'm not used to someone else dictating my life."

"And I'm sure you're not used to being shot at and attacked." Mustang tilted his head to the side, challenging her.

Emily sighed. "Point made." She turned to Grace.

Her friend grimaced. "I'm sorry, but I don't have another nightgown to loan you."

"I have a spare T-shirt," Mustang offered.

Emily nodded. "That'll do. Thank you."

"I guess, then, that we're calling it a night," Charlie said.

She turned to Emily. "I'm sorry this has happened to you on my property. I thought my security was pretty tight, but it seems that I wasn't prepared for a dump truck crashing into my stone wall. Nor did I conceive of someone infiltrating my house. I promise, I'll look through the security footage and determine from where he entered and shore up the locks."

Emily reached for Charlie's hands and squeezed them. "And I'm sorry I brought this trouble into your home."

Charlie waved a hand. "Don't you worry about us. We'll get things under control. That's why I hired Declan's Defenders."

Declan nodded. "Our main job right now is to keep you safe and to figure out who's attacking you."

Mustang frowned. "Not that we're doing such a great job so far."

Emily shook her head. "You are. I would be dead if you hadn't showed up when you did earlier. And you couldn't anticipate a breach in the estate security." Emily sighed. "I appreciate all your help in keeping me safe. Now, if you'll excuse me, I'm beyond tired." She turned and started for the door.

Mustang fell in step beside her and hooked his hand through her elbow. "I'm not trying to push you around. Consider it part of me just trying to do my job."

He climbed the stairs with her. When they reached the top, he walked with her to her bedroom. Once inside, he secured the French doors, locking the dead bolt. Then he checked the closets, beneath the bed and anywhere else someone might potentially hide. He even checked the cupboards and shower in the attached bathroom. When he was satisfied there were no other intruders in her room, he opened the adjoining door between his room and hers. "I'll get you that shirt," he said.

He gripped her arms, marched her across the room and positioned her in the doorway. "Stay right there."

Emily chuckled. "Isn't that taking it a little too far?"

"Not as far as I'm concerned," he said. "Last time I left you alone, you were pushed over a balcony."

Emily shivered. "I have to say, he did take me by surprise."

"And we thought the house was pretty secure." Mustang shook his head. "We can't assume anything." He walked to his go-bag, pulled out a T-shirt and handed it to her. "It's kind of ragged, but it's soft. It'll feel good against your skin."

She took the garment and pressed it against her cheek. "It is soft. I really appreciate it. At least I won't have to sleep in muddy clothes."

She turned and started to pull the adjoining door closed between their rooms.

Mustang caught the handle before she could completely close it. "Leave the door open," he said. "You can close the bathroom, but there are too many other entryways that can allow entry into your room. I would just as soon have my eyes on all of them."

She nodded, entered the bathroom and closed the door behind her.

Mustang waited until he heard the shower turn on. Then he walked into her room again and once more checked the windows, the French doors and the lock on her door to the hallway. He couldn't assume she was safe anywhere. If he didn't have his eyes on her, he had to know that there was no way anyone else could get to her.

While Emily showered, Mustang moved a wing-back chair up against the French doors leading out to the balcony. He pulled another chair from his room into hers and used it to block her bedroom door.

The shower turned off and a moment later Emily emerged, wearing his T-shirt and carrying the borrowed nightclothes. She had pulled her long blond hair into a messy bun on top of her head and there were droplets of water glistening on her shoulders and neck. Wearing his T-shirt, which came down over her thighs, she looked like a young girl in his oversize clothes. However, Mustang wasn't fooled. She was a full-grown woman with all the curves in all the right places. When she touched him, his senses went wild. Staring at her long, slender legs, all he could think about was wrapping those legs around his waist and—

Whoa! He couldn't go there. She was the job, not his next bed partner.

Emily stared at the two chairs. "Are we expecting another attack tonight?"

"No, but I want to be prepared in case one happens."

She nodded at the adjoining door that was closed. "I thought you'd leave the door open between our rooms, so you could keep an eye on me."

Mustang shook his head. "I won't be staying in there."

Emily's brows rose. "Uh, you're not sleeping with me."

He chuckled and nodded toward the chair leaning against the French doors. "I'm sleeping in that chair."

She frowned at the piece of furniture. "That won't be very comfortable."

"If I have any difficulties sleeping, I'll just stretch out on the floor. I've slept in worse places."

"That's right. You're a marine. I imagine you've slept in foxholes or out in the sand of the desert. Or beneath a tank or something like that." She grimaced. "I take it you've been deployed?"

He nodded. "A few times." He didn't bother to inform her that he'd been deployed over eighteen times to twelve different countries across the world. It might sound like bragging and he wasn't into bragging about what he did on active duty. He'd done what was asked of him. Guarding Emily was different. He hoped he didn't screw it up.

Chapter Eight

Emily slipped into the bed, climbed beneath the sheets, pulled the comforter up over her chest and stared at the man standing in front of her. "I mean, I know you are a marine. But what about before that?"

His mouth quirked upward on the corners. "What more do you want to know?"

She tilted her head and touched a finger to her chin. "How about...where did you grow up?"

"In Montana," he replied.

He wasn't going to help her with her interrogation. But Emily was persistent. "What did you do before the marines, in Montana?"

He crossed to the chair by the French doors and dropped down into it. "I was in high school like most kids my age."

Emily gave him a crooked grin. "You aren't going to make this easy, are you?"

His lips twisted into a wry grin. "Okay, so I grew up on a ranch."

Emily leaned forward. "Now we're getting somewhere." She raised her brows. "Go on. What part of Montana are you from? The open plains side or the mountains around Kalispell?"

Mustang tipped his head back against the chair's cushion and closed his eyes. "The nearest town to the ranch I grew up on was Cutbank. It's a town that's as close to Canada as you can get without actually being in Canada. But we didn't live there, we lived out on a ranch just south of that. It's on what they call the Front Range. Mostly plains, but we could see the mountains from my home." He raised his brows and opened his eyes to look across at her. "Does that help?"

Emily nodded. "It gives me an idea of where you're from anyway. So, I suppose, you ride horses?"

Mustang nodded. "I learned to ride before I learned to walk."

Emily's grin broadened. "Wow. Does that mean you're an honest-to-God, real-life cowboy?"

"If by *cowboy* you mean I know the difference between a horse and a cow, then, yes, I guess you could say I'm a cowboy."

"So, did you do all those things that cowboys do out West? You know, like branding and roping and herding the cattle?"

Mustang chuckled. "We did whatever it took to make sure the cattle were healthy and survived the brutal winters that they have out there on the plains in Montana."

"And then you joined the marines straight out of high school?"

Mustang nodded. "It's not like I would inherit the ranch when my parents pass away. My dad is the foreman of the ranch. I either had to sign on as a ranch hand or find another job. And since they had plenty of ranch hands, it was pretty much settled for me. The marines gave me an opportunity to get away from Montana and see the world."

As Emily stared across the room at Mustang, a thought occurred to her. "Do you have someone special in your life? Are you married? I mean, if you are, how are you going to explain sleeping in the same bedroom with another woman?"

Mustang chuckled. "I'm not married."

"Do you have a girlfriend or somebody you left behind in Montana?"

He shook his head. "No, I don't. The nature of the Marine Force Recon missions makes it so that it's hard to maintain a relationship when you could be deployed at any moment."

Emily frowned. "That has to be lonely."

"You don't have time to be lonely. And we have all our team to keep us company."

"I imagine the things you go through in the marines establishes a pretty strong bond between the men of your team," Emily said. "How long have you and your team been together? And are they the same ones you had when you were on active duty?"

"The men of Declan's Defenders are my teammates. Most of us have been together for the past four years. Jack Snow is the slack man—the newest member of the team. But even he's been with us for the past two years. They're my family now, my brothers. I'd take a bullet for any one of them."

"I imagine you would," Emily said.

"What about you?" Mustang asked.

"What about me?" Emily responded. "I don't know too many people I'd take a bullet for." She shrugged. "Although, I suppose I would for Grace."

Mustang shook his head. "No, I want to know more about you. Like, did you grow up on a ranch or did you grow up in the city?"

"My parents were older when they had me. They did the best they could to make sure I had a well-rounded upbringing. We lived in Virginia, in a suburb of DC." She smiled. "I learned to walk before I learned to ride a bicycle or ride a horse."

"So, you have ridden a horse?" Mustang asked.

"I have." Emily smiled. "Although it was purely through riding lessons. I've never owned my own horse. And we rode English not Western."

"That's more than some people have done. So many kids that grew up in the city have never even seen a horse in person. Yes, they've seen them on television, but they've never stood close to one, so you are fortunate in that respect."

"My parents did try to give me a good understanding of the world and everything in it. And that included a smattering of sports, which I was never very good at, and the riding lessons, which I enjoyed. I had hoped someday to have my own horse."

"And what's stopped you?"

"I live in the city." Emily shrugged. "The traffic and commute are awful. I wouldn't have time to really spend with a horse."

"Why DC? Why did you settle here?" Mustang asked.

Emily slipped down onto the pillow and yawned. "I don't know. I guess I just kind of slid in to the position at the university after completing my undergraduate degree, my masters and my doctorate there."

"You didn't want to explore the world and use your Russian language training in other parts of the country or the world?" Mustang asked.

Emily smiled. "I did study abroad for a semester in Moscow. And that was great, and I would really like to do some more traveling." She yawned again and stretched. "Just not tonight. The stress must have taken it out of me. I can't..." Emily closed her eyes as she yawned once more, hugely this time. "Sorry... I'm going to sleep now."

"Go ahead. I'll keep you safe while you do." He settled back, stretched his legs out in front of him and crossed his arms behind his head.

"Mmm." She nestled into the pillow, closing her eyes to a slit wide enough to study Mustang. He really was a handsome man. Too bad he was only there to keep her safe. He seemed a bit dangerous to her. At least to her libido. The man had charisma in spades. If she wasn't so darned tired, she might try to seduce him.

Another yawn nearly split her face in two.

Oh, who was she kidding? She didn't know how to seduce a man. So busy making good grades and then helping students make good grades and working as an interpreter, she hadn't taken the time out of her packed schedule to really learn the art of flirting much less dating.

Yeah, she'd gone out with a boy or two in college. She'd even experimented with sex. But she hadn't felt that certain "something" other women had claimed they'd felt. Perhaps her body wasn't built the same way as other women. Maybe she wasn't capable of feeling that special something during sex.

Another yawn made her eyes water. She couldn't fight it anymore. She had to let go of consciousness and sleep.

She recognized her hesitation and knew it had to do with all that had happened. She didn't want to dream about her attacker. Reliving the horrific experience was what nightmares were made of.

Knowing Mustang was only a few short steps away gave her a sense of relief. Finally she let go and drifted off into a dark abyss.

EMILY RAN, her breathing ragged, her lungs ready to burst. She didn't know where she was. All around her was a deep, inky blackness. And someone was chasing her.

Fear clutched at her chest, making it difficult to draw air into her lungs. But she had to keep moving.

Footsteps crunched on leaves and branches behind her.

Her foot caught on a root, pitching her forward. She landed hard in the dirt, the wind knocked from her lungs.

More footsteps sounded behind her.

Move! She had to move!

When she tucked her legs beneath her, they refused to push her to a standing position. With no strength left in her legs, she dragged herself up against a tree and curled into a ball, praying her pursuer couldn't find her. The darkness around her seemed to spin, sucking her downward. One moment she floated through space. The next she was falling...falling...falling.

Emily would have reached out her hands in search of something to hold on to, to break her fall, but she was afraid it would be him...

THE SOUND OF a soft cry jerked Mustang awake. He must have dozed off. His gaze shot to the bed and his heart froze in his chest.

Empty.

In a split second he shot to his feet and raced toward the door. The chair stood in the same place he'd positioned it. Reaching over the back of the chair, he gripped the handle, fully expecting the door to open easily, but the lock remained in place.

A keening moan sounded behind Mustang. He spun and his heart dropped to his knees.

Emily sat on the floor, wedged between the nightstand and the bed, her knees drawn up to her chest, her hands wrapped around her legs, and she was rocking back and forth. Another moan rose from her throat and a tear slipped from the corner of her eye.

"Oh, Emily," Mustang whispered. He hurried to her, switched on the light on the nightstand and dropped down beside her. "You're okay." He captured her hands in his and gently pulled her into his arms. "Hey, sweetheart, wake up."

She struggled, her body rigid, her hands pushing against his chest. "No. Please, no."

"It's okay," he crooned. "I won't let him hurt you."

Emily stopped fighting but her eyes remained closed.

"It's me, Mustang," he said. "Open your eyes. You're safe."

She shook her head, her fingers curling into his shirt.

"You're dreaming. Wake up and look at me." He chuckled, though it caught in his throat. "I'm one of the good guys."

Her eyelids fluttered and then opened. She stared up at him, blinking, a frown denting her smooth brow. Finally her eyes widened and she melted into his arms.

Mustang wrapped her in his embrace, smoothing his hands down her back. "You're all right. It was just a bad dream. I'm here. I won't let anyone hurt you."

"He was chasing me. I tr-tripped." She dragged in a shaky breath and let it out.

The warmth of her exhalation spread across Mustang's chest. He held her closer and swept his hand over her hair, cupping the back of her head.

She leaned back far enough that she could look up into his eyes. "Thank you."

He shook his head. "For what?"

"For saving me again," Emily said, and laid her cheek against his chest, snuggling closer against him.

"I didn't do anything but wake you up."

"It was enough." She slipped her arms around his waist and held on, as if she might fall if she let go.

Mustang shifted, pulling her into his lap. For a long time he sat there, holding her until her body relaxed against his. She was warm and soft against him, and her hair smelled of flowers and springtime. His T-shirt on her body did little to disguise her curves pressed against his torso and chest.

His groin tightened. Now was not a good time to be turned on by the woman he was there to protect. She didn't need her bodyguard making a pass at her.

But he couldn't control his body's reaction. And if he didn't move soon, she'd become aware of his lack of control.

"We should get you off the floor," he whispered against her ear, fighting the urge to nibble at her lobe.

Her arms tightened around his middle. For a long moment she didn't say anything. Slowly she loosened her hold around him and nodded. "Okay."

He shifted her off his lap and rose. Instead of reaching a hand down to pull her to a standing position, he bent, scooped her up in his arms and lifted her onto the bed.

She clung to him until he settled her on the comforter. "I could have gotten here on my own," she reminded him. "But thank you." Emily leaned forward and kissed his cheek. Her eyes widened and she dropped back against the pillow. "Sorry. I shouldn't have done that."

Mustang's face tingled where Emily's lips had touched. He pressed his fingers to the spot and gave her a crooked smile. "I didn't mind."

Her cheeks reddened. "Still, I shouldn't

have." She snuggled under the sheets then pulled them and the comforter up to her chin and stared at him, her eyes wide.

"You can leave the light on. It won't bother me," Mustang said. He turned toward his chair.

"Mustang?" Emily said, her voice little more than a whisper.

He could hear the desperation and fear lacing the sweet sound of his name on her lips. Without hesitation, he turned back to her. "Yes?"

She chewed on her bottom lip before answering, "Will you stay with me?"

He nodded. "I'm not going anywhere. I'll be in that chair, all night long."

Emily shook her head. "No. Here." She moved over, making room for him on the queen-size bed.

He stared at her and the space beside her and swallowed a groan. "I don't know. That might not be a good idea."

She shrank back against the pillow. "Oh. Okay. I'm sorry. I shouldn't have asked. It's just…when I close my eyes, I'm afraid I'll end up right back in that dream." Her voice faded at the end. With a little more oomph, she added, "It's okay. I'll manage." And she turned over, away from him. "Good night, Mustang," she said.

Mustang stood for a long time, reminding

himself he was being paid to watch out for this woman, not to sleep with her. His jeans tightened uncomfortably. Lying in bed with Emily could only be painful and make for a very long, sleepless night. Even more so than sleeping in the chair.

He straightened his shoulders.

No. He should walk away and keep his distance from her. They'd been strangers before that night. They'd be strangers when the threat was neutralized. He didn't need to start anything that would go nowhere. Not that lying in bed with her meant he had her permission to start something.

He started toward the chair, stopped, spun and crossed to the bed. Kicking off his shoes, he stretched out beside Emily on the bed, lying on top of the comforter.

Emily drew in a deep breath and let it out on a sigh. "Thank you."

For a long time Mustang lay staring at the ceiling, his body hard, his fists clenched.

He was just about to slide out of the bed and return to his chair when Emily rolled over and slid an arm across his chest.

Swallowing hard to keep from groaning, Mustang froze.

Emily pressed her cheek against the side of

his chest, her eyes closed, her breathing steady and relaxed.

He couldn't move. What scared him worst was…he didn't want to. He liked having her body next to his. He wanted to hold her all through the night. What scared him even more was he had a feeling one night wouldn't be long enough.

Chapter Nine

Emily woke to sunshine streaming through a window, cutting across the floor and edging beneath the slits of her closed eyes. She blinked them open, winced and closed them again. On her second attempt, she was able to open her eyes fully and welcome the morning with a smile.

She stretched, her arm falling across the opposite side of the bed. It was empty.

Sometime during the night or early morning Mustang had left the bed. The bathroom door stood halfway open and she could hear water running in the sink. Emily rolled onto her side.

Through the gap in the door, she could see him.

Mustang stood shirtless at the sink, smearing shaving cream over his chin.

Emily's breath lodged in her throat and her pulse pounded through her veins.

The man had broad, tanned shoulders. From

where she lay, she could see the evidence of scars on his arms and side. They didn't detract at all from his rugged good looks. In fact, they made her heart flutter and warmth spread low in her belly.

He'd held her in his arms when she'd been frightened by a dream. Then she'd taken advantage of him by asking him to lie beside her in the bed. She had no regrets in that regard. Having his hard body beside hers had chased away all the bad guys of her imagination and made her feel safe and protected.

She'd slept the rest of the night without a recurrence of the horrible nightmare. With sun shining through the window, she met the day with more optimism than she'd had the night before. And more determination to discover who was behind the attacks. She suspected it had something to do with her visit to the Russian embassy. Had the situation with the ambassador's daughter caused such a stir they didn't want the information to leak out? Emily shook her head. Why would they need to keep that such a secret? Who cared besides the ambassador?

Mustang finished shaving and tapped the razor on the side of the sink. Then he turned his head toward her and winked. "Caught ya looking."

Heat flared in Emily's cheeks and she rolled back to her side of the bed. Her bare feet hit the cool wooden floor. She searched the room for her clothes before she remembered they had been covered in mud and too nasty to wear again. The sweatpants and T-shirt Grace had loaned her were gone as well.

"If you're looking for clothes, you'll find the items you arrived in stacked on the dresser. Charlie had them cleaned while you slept."

Relief washed over her as she gathered her pants, shirt, panties and bra. When she started toward the adjoining door, intent on changing out of the revealing T-shirt, she was brought up short by Mustang clearing his throat.

"Ahem. Where are you going?"

She spun to face him, clutching the stack of clothing to her chest. "To change into my clothes."

"If you go into my room and close the door, I won't be able to see you, or protect you against an intruder entering that room." He tipped his head toward the bathroom behind him. "I'm done in here."

She nodded and hurried forward, intent on giving him a wide berth, knowing if she touched him, she'd feel that spark of electricity he managed to generate without trying.

As she walked past him, he reached out a hand and touched her arm.

Emily fought hard not to moan. She came to a halt, gathered her scattered senses and looked up into Mustang's eyes questioningly.

"How do you feel this morning?" he asked, his tone low, intimate and far too sexy for Emily's good.

Those scattered senses scrambled all over again. She struggled to concentrate on what he'd said while staring at his lips, wondering what they would feel like against hers. She shook her head. "Fine," she blurted. "I'm fine." Then she scurried into the bathroom. Once she'd closed the door between them, she leaned against it and let go of the breath she'd been holding.

Why was she so rattled by the man? He was there to protect her, but she was afraid. Not of him, but of her uncontrolled reaction to him. She was nothing more to him than a person he'd been hired to protect. He wasn't there because he was in love with her. The measure of his success on the job was to keep her alive, not to make love to her.

A moan escaped her lips at the idea of making love with the man.

Emily hurried to the sink, turned on the cold water and splashed it into her face.

The shock of the icy water helped bring her back to earth. She scrubbed her face, found a packaged toothbrush under the sink and scrubbed the night's funk off her teeth. She ran a brush through her hair, pulled on her own blouse and pants and felt more in control of her body and mind.

Squaring her shoulders, she braced herself for her next encounter with Mustang. With a deep breath Emily flung open the door, fully expecting to face the man who occupied all of her thoughts.

The room was empty.

A moment of panic flashed through her.

She hurried to the adjoining door into his room.

Mustang stepped in front of her.

"Did you miss me?"

She pressed a hand against his chest and let go of the breath she'd been holding, steadying herself. "No, of course not," she lied.

"Do you always lose your breath walking across the room?"

Emily struggled to come up with some excuse for her reaction to thinking he'd gone.

"I just… I just…" She sighed. "Yes, I missed you."

His lips twisted as he opened his arms. "Come here."

She didn't hesitate. She walked into his arms and rested her cheek against his chest. The steady sound of his heartbeat soothed her immediately. "I thought you'd left."

"Sweetheart, I told you I wasn't leaving you out of my sight."

"But then you were gone," she pointed out.

She stood in the circle of his arms inhaling the scent of his aftershave.

He had put on a polo shirt, tucked it into his jeans and combed his hair.

Even with all those lovely muscles covered, he felt like a solid brick wall.

He flexed his shoulders naturally.

Mustang settled a finger beneath her chin and tipped her head upward. "Hey, I'm not leaving you." He pressed his lips to her forehead. "I'm sticking with you, girl."

"Promise?"

He nodded and lowered his face to brush his lips across hers.

Before he could lift his head, she captured his cheeks between her hands and stood on her toes to press her lips more firmly to his.

His hands slid up her back and cupped her head, bringing her closer to deepen the kiss.

When at last he lifted his head, he stared down into her eyes. "I shouldn't have done that. But I'm not sorry."

Emily shook her head. "I shouldn't have kissed you back."

A knock sounded on the door. "Emily?" Grace's voice rang through the paneling.

Emily stepped back.

Mustang's arms fell to his sides.

"I'm awake," Emily said.

"Breakfast is ready, if you'd like to join us," Grace said.

Emily stared into Mustang's eyes. "I'll be down in a moment."

"Great. See you there," Grace called out. Footsteps sounded, leading away from the door.

Emily took another slight step back. "We'd better go."

Mustang hesitated. "Emily..."

Emily held up a hand. "Let's just leave it here."

He took a step closer. "What if I don't want to leave it here?"

She took a deep breath and let it out slowly. "We should go down."

"I shouldn't have kissed you," Mustang said. "But I couldn't help myself.

"Ditto." Emily shook her head. "It just... complicates things."

He shoved a hand through his hair. "I get it. And your life is pretty complicated right now."

Emily nodded.

He stared at Emily for a long moment. "Then let's uncomplicate this. I'll stay as far away as possible, as long as I can still be effective protecting you." Mustang moved the chair away from the door, unlocked it and opened the door. "After you."

Emily led the way down the stairs and followed the sound of voices coming from the dining room. She wasn't certain how Mustang would stay away from her, if he had to be right beside her to protect her. And she didn't want him to go far. Not with all that had happened. He was her rock in a turbulent sea. She wasn't combat trained and she didn't have any self-defense skills to fight off an attacker.

DECLAN, GRACE, CHARLIE and Arnold the butler were there. Sitting around the dining table. Plates of sausage, eggs, bacon, hash browns and toast lined the middle of the table. Emily's stomach rumbled. She hadn't realized just how hungry she was.

"Glad you could join us," Charlie said. "I trust you slept well?"

Emily didn't bother to tell Charlie about her bad dream or the fact that Mustang had slept with her. Instead she nodded as she took a seat beside Grace. Mustang sat next to Emily.

"Are you still good with the plan we have for today?" Declan asked.

Emily glanced around at the others at the table. "I am. I have a class to teach today. After that I'd like to go with you to talk to the private investigator."

"I had Cole run a background investigation on your private investigator. We didn't find anything unusual. He did do some time in the military in the NCIS." Declan nodded. "What time do you think you will be done with your class?"

"I should be finished by noon."

"I'm not sure it's a good idea for you to be walking around the city. Especially since we don't know who is trying to attack you," Declan said.

"I can't just hide away and wait until my problem goes away," Emily said.

"You put yourself at risk." Declan nodded to Mustang. "I'm not sure one bodyguard will be enough."

"I hate that anybody has to be my bodyguard," Emily admitted.

"I'm sure you didn't ask to be attacked," Mustang said.

"Well, we don't mind providing your protection," Charlie said. "The local police are investigating, but it's clear whoever is after you is persistent and resourceful."

"As long as the boss lady says so, we'll provide that protection," Declan told her.

"Correction, I'll be here whether the boss lady says so or not," Mustang said.

Tears welled in Emily's eyes. "Thank you all. I feel so much safer just knowing that you have my back."

"That goes for all of us," Grace said. "We're here for you, Emily."

Emily scooped eggs onto her plate, a piece of bacon and a piece of toast. And then she watched as Mustang loaded his plate with eggs, toast, hash browns, sausage and bacon. And proceeded to consume all.

She picked at her breakfast and drank a small glass of orange juice before she finally pushed her plate away and scooted her chair from the table. "I need to go by my apartment before I go to the university."

Mustang shoved the last bite of his toast into his mouth before pushing back from the table and standing. "I'm ready to go."

"Do you want us to go with you?" Grace said, glancing over at Declan.

"No, I think it will be enough of a disturbance to have one bodyguard in the classroom along with the rest of the students," Emily said, shooting a glance at Mustang.

The former marine would have every student in the classroom wondering why he was there and if he was single. At least the female students. And half of the male students, as well.

"I'll have your car towed to the body shop," Charlie told Emily.

"Thank you." Emily smiled at Charlie. "You've already done so much for me. I'm sure insurance will help with the repairs, if the car is not totaled."

"My guy's a good repairman," Charlie said. "I'll have him give me an estimate."

"Either way," Emily conceded, "I'll be out of a vehicle at least for a couple of weeks. I guess I'd better look into a rental car."

Mustang frowned. "I don't know why you need a rental car as long as you have me. We'll go in my truck."

"You can't be with me all the time," Emily said.

"That's exactly what I will be. With you. All the time." Mustang crossed his arms over his chest. "Until we figure out who your attacker is, and we neutralize him, you're with me 24/7."

"Surely, you have a life of your own?" Emily said.

"Get this," Mustang stressed. "You are my life. Period. Period. Period."

Emily shook her head.

Mustang held up a hand. "Until we get this attacker in hand, you are my only job. We will eat, drink and sleep together as long as we need to."

Heat rushed into Emily's cheeks and she glanced around the room at the others. Grace had a half smile tugging at her lips.

Declan nodded, a serious look on his face. "Mustang's right."

Grace nodded. "He is. We'll all feel better if he's with you 24/7."

"And we'll add additional bodyguards as needed," Charlie offered.

"It seems like so much trouble," Emily said.

Mustang held up his hand again. "End of argument," he said. "Are you ready to go?"

Emily valued her independence, but what they were saying was right. She needed them until they found the attacker and put him away. She nodded. "All right. But no entourage. Just Mustang and me. I'm ready. Let's go."

MUSTANG MADE EMILY wait at the door as he stepped outside. He searched the surrounding area quickly before ushering her out to his truck. He used his body as a shield between her and any potential threat. When he had her settled in the passenger seat, he closed the door and rounded the front of the vehicle to climb into the driver's seat.

With Emily's direction, he maneuvered through the traffic of DC to Arlington, where her apartment was located. When they arrived at her building, he pulled into the parking lot slowly, his gaze scanning the immediate surroundings.

"You can wait in the truck while I go inside and gather a few things," Emily said.

"Nope," Mustang said. "We're both going in." He shifted one hand under his jacket where he kept his Glock in a shoulder holster. Then he dropped down from the truck, rounded to the other side, opened the door and helped Emily to the ground. He kept her in the curve of his other arm, protecting her with his body as they hurried toward the apartment building.

When they stopped in front of her apartment, Emily fumbled with her key until she finally got it into the lock, twisted it and opened the door.

Mustang kept Emily from walking in by placing a hand on her arm. He drew his weapon and pushed the door wider. After a quick glance around the exterior of her apartment, he entered and tugged her in behind him.

Once inside, Mustang pulled the door closed behind Emily with a soft click. He pressed a finger to his lips, pointed to the corner by the door and then pointed at her. He mouthed the word *Stay*.

Emily frowned but nodded and took up her position in the corner.

Mustang would have preferred to clear her apartment before allowing her to enter, but he couldn't leave her outside for fear somebody might attack her while he was busy searching the apartment. With no other choice, he'd had to bring her in and plant her by the front door while he cleared the rest of the apartment.

He entered the main living area, scanning for any sign of an intruder. The room was sparsely but tastefully furnished with a light gray, modern sofa, a white marble-topped coffee table with matching end tables on either side of the sofa, and a white leather chair and ottoman. Bright red, orange and turquoise pillows provided splashes of color to an otherwise gray-and-white interior. One wall contained an Impressionist painting of a summer wheat field with a bright blue sky. On another wall were black-and-white photographs of bridges, each had been enlarged and printed on canvas.

On an end table was a photograph of a family of three. Emily was front and center between an older man and woman. Mustang assumed they were her parents. He absorbed the decorations in a brief scan as he moved through the living room and into the kitchen. Once he was sure there weren't any bogeys hiding behind the sofa or in the pantry, he entered the bedroom—a room as different from the living room as night was to day. In this room, the bed was covered in a blush pink comforter with a stack of fluffy pillows pushed up against a white-cushioned headboard. The dresser was of a light, whitewashed wood with brushed, stainless-steel pulls.

The painting hanging over the bed was of a young girl wearing an old-fashioned hat and a long white dress. She was carrying a basketful of wildflowers. The entire room was utterly feminine and what he would have expected of Emily. Soft…delicate…and vulnerable. His chest tightened. Mustang didn't like that she was being targeted. He vowed to keep her safe, no matter the cost to himself.

There weren't too many places a person could hide. But he checked them all, looking under the bed, in the closet and behind the shower curtain. When he was convinced there were no other people in the apartment besides him and Emily he called out, "All clear."

Emily entered the bedroom and stared across

the floor at him. "Do I have to worry about every place I go?"

Mustang nodded. "Afraid so."

Emily's frown was more sad than angry. She made quick work of finding a small suitcase and stuffing it full of clothes that she might need for the next week. She entered the bathroom and collected toiletries, putting them into a smaller case that fit within her suitcase. When she finished, she zipped the case, lifted it off the bed and set it on the floor. "I just need to gather my book bag and then I'll be ready to go."

Back in the living room she gathered a stack of papers, shoved them into a satchel and looped the strap of the bag over her shoulder.

Mustang carried her suitcase to the door and waited patiently.

Emily's gaze swept the apartment, ending up connecting with Mustang's. "I don't like it."

Mustang nodded. "I understand. Nobody likes it when their personal space is invaded. Or even if their personal space has the risk of being invaded."

Emily shivered. "I feel like I have to be looking over my shoulder every step I take."

"And that's exactly what you have to do. Until we find the attacker," Mustang said.

She squared her shoulders and marched toward the door. "Then let's go. I have a class to teach."

Once again, Mustang was out the door first, checking the parking lot for any vehicles that may have arrived while they were inside or any people that looked suspect. When he felt certain all was clear, he looped his arm around Emily's shoulder, pulled her close to his body and guided her toward the truck.

For the next thirty minutes he contended with DC traffic to get Emily to the university in time for her class to begin. Once they arrived on campus, Mustang parked the truck in a parking garage and went around to let Emily out. They arrived at her classroom with no interference.

Mustang was surprised by the size of the space. It wasn't so much a classroom as it was an auditorium, albeit a small one, with about two dozen students seated among the one hundred or more chairs.

They entered from the back of the auditorium.

Emily paused and touched a hand to his arm. "I'd prefer if you stayed in the back," she whispered. "Having a stranger in the classroom is enough of a distraction with you being in my face or following me everywhere."

He frowned, studying the room of students. "Do you recognize all of these people?"

She nodded. "All have been in my class from the beginning of the semester." Emily smiled. "They aren't here to hurt me. They're here to learn to speak Russian."

Mustang didn't like that she would be all the way across the room from him. "Is there another door leading into the room near the front?"

Emily shook her head. "Only the ones here at the rear of the classroom." She glanced at the double doors. "I'd feel safer and more comfortable if you guarded the doors rather than guarding me."

"Are these all of the students?" he asked. "Are you expecting more?"

She nodded. "I have exactly twenty-five students. I did a quick count. They're all here." She nodded toward a young man standing near the front of the class. "The student standing is my teacher's assistant. He's enrolled in the masters-level program. He will help me to administer the test."

After one more glance around the room at the students, Mustang nodded. "Okay. But if I say 'hit the ground,' I expect you to drop to your belly." He gave her a fierce glance. "Got that?"

She held up her hand as if swearing an oath, the corners of her lips quirking. "Got it."

"Okay then, go teach." He stood in front of the door, his arms crossed over his chest. He wouldn't allow anyone else to enter the room without going through him. And if one of the students tried to make a move on Emily, Mustang could be across the room in seconds.

For the next hour Emily conducted a last-minute review, speaking in Russian and in English.

Mustang was entranced by her smooth, sexy voice and the way the Russian language rolled off her lips as if she'd been born to speak it.

If he had only been mildly attracted to her before, he now found himself completely under her spell.

By the look of some of the male students, they were equally captivated. The woman was smart, sexy, and didn't appear to be much older than her students. Some raised their hands and asked questions. She responded with a smile and clearly enunciated words. Emily knew her stuff. No wonder she was in demand as an interpreter.

After the hour was over, she asked her students to put away their books and get out their pencils.

Her teacher's assistant handed out the scanner test forms while Emily distributed the actual tests, face-down.

Once each student had a form and a test, Emily walked to the front of the class, glanced at her watch and then looked up. "You have one hour to complete the test. You may begin."

For the next hour the students worked through their tests at their own paces. By the end of the hour, they trickled up to the front of the room, handed over their completed forms and the test, and left, walking past Mustang as they went. Male and female students only gave him a brief glance as they exited. They appeared to be deep in thought, as if second-guessing their answers.

When the hour ended and there were still students at their tables, working on their tests, Emily cleared her throat.

"Time's up," she called out. "Put down your pencils and bring your tests and answer sheets to me."

The remaining handful of students submitted their papers and left the room.

Emily and her assistant stacked the tests and the scanner forms. After Emily tucked them into her satchel, she thanked the assistant and told him he could leave.

The assistant brushed past Mustang, eyebrows raised. But the young man didn't comment. Instead he left, letting the door swing closed behind him.

"I need to take my forms to my office and run them through the test-scanning software." Emily looped the satchel's strap over her shoulder and started up the aisle toward Mustang. "The students will want to know their grades as soon as possible. Then we can go see Jay Phillips, the private investigator."

Mustang nodded and held out his hands. "Do you want me to carry anything?"

Emily smiled and shook her head. "No need. I do this all the time." When she started to pass him, he put out his arm.

"Let me go first."

With a sigh, she hung back.

Before Mustang could put his hand out to open the door, it burst outward.

He shoved Emily behind him and dropped into a ready crouch, his hand going to the gun beneath his jacket. He had it pulled and pointed at the intruder before she was completely inside the classroom.

The young woman stood no more than approximately five feet tall with pitch-black hair, ice-blue eyes and pale skin. She stopped short, the door swinging closed behind her. "Oh!" she said and took a step backward, raising her hands, her eyes wide and frightened. "I'm not here to hurt Miss Chastain," she said with a heavy Russian accent. "I need her help."

Mustang refused to move. "Who are you and what do you want with Miss Chastain?"

The woman shot a nervous glance over her shoulder. "Please," she said softly. "If they find me, I won't be able to speak freely. I need to talk to Miss Chastain." She held up her hands higher. "I am not armed."

Emily touched Mustang's arm. "Let her talk."

"She might not have a gun, but she could be carrying a knife."

"You can…how you say? Frisk me. But please, away from the door. If my bodyguards find me, they will take me back to the embassy."

Emily stepped around Mustang. "The Russian embassy?"

The woman nodded, shot another glance over her shoulder. "I told my father I wanted to enroll in classes. I ran away from my bodyguards. It is only moments before they find me." She pressed her hands together. "Please, I must speak with you, Miss Chastain. It is a matter of life and death."

Chapter Ten

"You must be Sachi," Emily said and moved forward.

Mustang shot out his arm to keep Emily from stepping past him.

"It's okay," Emily said. "Sachi is Russian Ambassador Nikolai Kozlov's daughter." When she tried to lower his arm, it remained firm.

"You can't trust anyone," Mustang said. "Not even another woman."

"Miss Kozlov won't hurt me," Emily said and turned to Sachi. "Will you?"

Sachi stared at Emily wide-eyed. "No, no. Of course not."

"Still, I'd rather make certain she isn't carrying a weapon."

Sachi held out her arms and spread her feet apart. "Please hurry. If my bodyguards find me, I will not have another chance to speak to Miss Chastain."

Mustang ran his hands lightly over her arms,

along her sides, down to her shoes and then checked inside her jacket. When he was done, he stepped back and allowed Emily to move forward. "She's clean."

Emily closed the distance between her and Sachi.

Sachi moved away from the door into a corner of the classroom while Emily flipped one of the light switches near the entrance, plunging that corner into darkness. Then she followed Sachi, with Mustang close behind. "What is it you wanted to discuss?"

Sachi glanced over Emily's shoulder toward the door before she spoke. "My father has made it impossible for me to get out of the embassy alone. He treats me like a child, when I am twenty-six years old."

SACHI COLLAPSED AGAINST EMILY, sobbing. Emily wrapped her arms around Sachi and looked over her head into Mustang's eyes.

"Is your love the journalist Tyler Blunt?" Emily asked.

"Yes," Sachi said. "He is. And my father is furious. He thinks Tyler is a risk to his position as the ambassador."

"Why does he think that?" Emily asked.

"He thinks Tyler is only seeing me so he can

get bad information about what the Russians are doing in the United States."

"And do you think Tyler is using you?" Emily asked.

"No, of course not." Sachi shook her head. "Tyler loves me."

Emily didn't bother telling the young Russian girl that journalists sometimes could be quite crooked and start relationships with people just to use them for a story. What good would it do when Emily knew nothing of Tyler's true intentions?

Sachi frowned and stared into Emily's eyes. "You don't believe me, do you?"

"I didn't say that," Emily said. "Question is, what do you want me to do about it?"

"My father said he hired a private investigator to follow Tyler," Sachi said. "Who was the private investigator?"

"I'm not at liberty to reveal anything about my conversation with your father," Emily said.

Sachi grabbed her hands and squeezed. "Please, you need to tell me. I think the private investigator might have seen something. Might know something about what Tyler was working on. Maybe he knows something about why Tyler disappeared."

Emily shook her head. "I signed a nondisclosure agreement with your father. If you want to know who the private investigator is, why don't you ask your father?"

"He won't tell me," Sachi said.

Again Emily shook her head. "I'm sorry, I just can't tell you."

More tears welled in Sachi's eyes. "It could be the difference in life and death for Tyler," she said. "What if he's been kidnapped? What if he is being tortured?"

Emily pressed her lips together. "Talk to your dad. I can't say anything."

Sachi dropped Emily's hands, turned and paced a few steps away. Turned and came back. "Tyler said he was working on a project that could have some very serious ramifications. He seemed nervous about it. He thought it was really dangerous."

"Did he say anything about what it was?"

Sachi shook her head. "He didn't want me to know. Not until he had all the details."

"And you think this project that he was working on may have gotten him in trouble?"

Sachi nodded. She ran a hand through her rich black hair and sighed. "I wish he would have told me what the project was. Then at least I would have some kind of place to start looking for him."

Standing in the shadows with the Russian ambassador's daughter, Emily could feel the tension and the fear. If the man she loved had disappeared like Tyler Blunt had disappeared, she, too, would be searching for answers. But she couldn't violate her nondisclosure.

Emily sighed. "Sachi, I can't tell you who the investigator was. That information you will have to get from your father. However, I can check with him and see if he knows anything." She had been going to go talk with the private investigator anyway. It wouldn't hurt, and it wouldn't violate the nondisclosure agreement for her to talk to the investigator. Especially now that she knew who he had been talking about during the interpretation session—Tyler Blunt.

Sachi grasped her hands once again. She stared at Emily. "Please, you will tell me if you learn anything about where Tyler might be?"

Emily nodded. "I'll tell you what I can. But I'll need some way to contact you."

Sachi took a business card from her wallet. She pulled a pen from her purse and wrote a phone number on the back of the card. "Call me if you learn anything."

Emily reciprocated and gave Sachi her number, as well.

Heavy footsteps sounded in the hallway. Sachi heaved a frustrated sigh. "I have to get back to my bodyguards. My father will be angry when he finds that they lost me. I can take his anger. But it isn't fair to the bodyguards when he gets angry."

"Will you be all right?" Emily asked.

Sachi nodded. "As well as can be expected. I will not rest until I find Tyler."

She squeezed Emily's hands one more time before she released them, turned and hurried toward the exit doors. As she reached out to open them, they pushed outward and two burly, heavyset men entered.

Mustang started after Sachi.

Emily's hand shot out and grabbed his arm.

The ambassador's daughter spoke in fluent Russian to the two men. They responded also in Russian. And soon all three left the auditorium. Mustang's gaze followed Sachi out the door. He turned to Emily. "I'd follow her to make sure she's all right, but that would leave you exposed."

Emily shook her head. "She knew the men. She spoke to them as if she had a long-standing relationship with them as her bodyguards."

"Still, she looked scared."

Emily nodded. "She is scared. But not for herself, for her lover, the journalist Tyler Blunt." Emily shook her head.

"Let me guess, you want to go talk to Jay Phillips now?" Mustang said.

Emily's eyes narrowed. "You bet. Your team wanted to follow up with him today anyway. So, we'll do it."

"Okay," Mustang said. "I'll let Declan know we'll handle it."

"And then we can stop by the office that hired me to translate for the embassy." She met Mustang's gaze. "With as much trouble as I've been having lately, do you think Sachi is in trouble, as well?"

Mustang shrugged. "I don't know. But she has two bodyguards. They should keep her safe."

"I'm kind of worried about her," Emily said. "Do you think her father had something to do with Tyler Blunt's disappearance?"

Emily's lips pressed tightly together. "I don't know, but it's all pretty suspicious. Considering I saw Blunt being led deeper into the embassy instead of out of it."

"Sounds to me like the Russians had something to do with Mr. Blunt's disappearance."

Emily nodded. "You should have seen how mad the ambassador was when he found out that his daughter had been having an affair with the man Jay Phillips had been tasked to follow."

"All the more reason for us to get to this

private investigator and ask a few questions of our own."

Emily nodded, slipped her satchel more firmly over her shoulder and started for the door. Mustang beat her to it and stepped outside first. After he had checked both directions of the hallway, he opened the door for her and led her out of the building and back to the lot where he had parked his truck.

He had just settled Emily in her seat when a loud bang sounded, echoing off the walls of the parking garage. Glass shattered the passenger window of his truck just as she was bending over to retrieve a paper that had fallen from her satchel. Instinct took over as he shoved Emily sideways in the front seat and then crouched low behind the metal of the door. Another shot rang out, hitting the front windshield.

Emily shuttered her hand out. "Give me your truck keys," she said.

"Why?" Mustang asked.

"Just do it," she demanded.

He handed her the keys. She scrambled across the console into the driver's seat. "Get in," she ordered.

Another shot pierced the front and back windshields leaving small holes with cracks like spider's legs reaching out. Emily jammed the key into the ignition and turned on the engine.

Mustang scrambled up into the passenger seat and closed the door, still remaining low, out of range of the windshields.

Emily slammed the gearshift into Reverse. She backed out of the parking space, shifted into Drive and hit the accelerator, shooting the truck forward toward the exit. She didn't let the fear of being shot slow her down. She kept her foot on the accelerator, taking turns in the parking garage at a much too fast pace to make her comfortable. But she had to get out of there before someone finally hit their target. Her.

While Emily navigated getting out of the parking garage alive, Mustang was on his cell phone dialing 9-1-1. "I'd like to report an active shooter on campus at the university."

Emily was so angry at herself as she pulled out of the garage and onto the campus street. If she hadn't showed up that day, insisting her students needed to take their tests to get the grade for class, the campus would not have had an active shooter. She was in trouble and had brought that trouble to the campus, putting the students at risk.

As she left campus she vowed not to return until her attacker was captured and put behind bars. She'd get her test results in electronically somehow.

MUSTANG HAD INSISTED Emily keep going until they were miles away from the university campus. He didn't want to stop at all, but he knew they would have to file some kind of report with the police since he had called in the active shooter. He was proud of Emily for keeping a level head and getting them out of the parking garage and off the campus. She was still driving at a fairly fast rate, at the same time not erratic enough to run over pedestrians. He looked back every few minutes to make sure they were not being followed. When he felt certain they were safe, he had her pull over at a gas station, where they arranged for the police to come and question them about the incident.

After Mustang gave his statement to the police, he placed a call to Declan and explained their situation.

"I'm glad you got out of there alive," Declan said.

Mustang glanced over at Emily. "So am I, dude. So am I."

"Do you need me to send another one of the guys out to help protect Emily?" Declan asked. "Or Mack and I can interview Phillips."

Mustang debated taking Declan up on his offer, but they needed to talk with the private investigator, and he might get spooked if there were too many people bombarding him at once. "No, I think we need to do this, just me and Emily."

"Fair enough," Declan said.

"What I need from you and the others is information. Give me the address of this private investigator, Jay Phillips."

"I'm on my way to you," Declan said, "and I'm texting you Phillips's address. Good luck getting information from him. Most investigators don't share private data of the people they investigate. Of course, unless you're the one paying him to do the investigation."

"I don't know why they're targeting me," Emily said as she wrapped her arms around her middle and moved closer to Mustang. "Nothing in that report seems worth all this."

He put his arm around her. "You're safe with me and my team," he said into her hair. "I won't let you down."

Chapter Eleven

Minutes later Declan joined Mustang and Emily at the service station as the police wrapped up their investigation.

"Thought you might need another vehicle," Declan said. He tipped his head at a dark gray sedan pulling into the parking lot. "Charlie sent a backup car. She could have sent a truck, but she said this one blended more easily into the DC traffic."

Mustang shot a glance toward his pickup with the bullet holes in the windshield and side windows. His stomach roiled. Any one of those bullets could have hit Emily. "Tell Charlie thanks." His gaze shifted to Emily. "It might be a good idea to take Emily back to the Halverson estate. She's not safe out here."

Emily shook her head even before he finished speaking. "I'm not going to sit back at Charlie's and wait for the trouble to miraculously disappear. I want to have a word with

Jay Phillips. And if that isn't any help, I'm going to request a meeting with the Russian ambassador. I have to get to the bottom of this." As she spoke, her anger became more evident and a bright fire burned in her eyes.

Mustang couldn't help but think how very sexy she was when riled. He chuckled. "Okay. You're staying with me. But we might need to get you into a bulletproof vest."

"Whatever it takes," she said.

Mack climbed out of the dark gray sedan and handed the keys to Mustang. "She's all yours while your truck in is the shop."

"Good." Mustang cupped the keys in his palm. He filled Declan and Mack in on the rest of the details of their encounter with Sachi Kozlov.

"So, she was having an affair with Tyler Blunt." Declan shook his head. "I can understand her concerns. From what Cole has learned, the man has yet to turn up."

"I know he's the one I saw in the Russian embassy," Emily said. "Surely they wouldn't have done something stupid like kill the man on American soil."

"You would think they wouldn't have done it at the embassy," Mustang said.

"Perhaps that's why they want Emily out of the picture," Mack said. "She saw Blunt there.

She could call them out and have the embassy investigated for kidnapping and potentially for murder."

Mustang frowned. "You wouldn't think having an affair with the ambassador's daughter would be enough to make the Russians want to kill the journalist."

"You didn't see how mad the ambassador was," Emily said. "He stormed out of the conference room shouting obscenities. His face was red and there were veins popping out on his forehead. I don't think I've seen anyone quite that mad."

"Well, since we can't find the journalist, we'll have to settle for the other American in that session with the ambassador," Declan said.

"The address you gave me…is it his home or office?" Mustang asked.

Declan snorted. "His home." He pulled his smartphone from his pocket and clicked some buttons. "I just sent you a text with the office address, too, so you have it. Mack and I will go by his office. You and Emily can swing by his home. We tried calling his work number, but got no response. He might be there, but he's not answering. Same with his home number."

Mustang nodded. "We'll head for his house. Hopefully he can shed some light on what's going on."

"*If* we find him," Emily murmured. "Alive."

Declan climbed into his truck. Mack joined him. They took off in the direction of Phillips's office.

Mustang held the door for Emily and waited while she slipped into the sedan. Then he slid behind the steering wheel, adjusted the seat and mirrors and pulled out into the traffic. He followed the directions given by the map application on his cell phone. Twenty minutes later he pulled into the driveway of a modest town house with a one-car garage.

Just by looking at the building, he couldn't tell if anyone was home. The shades were drawn and the garage door was closed.

He stepped out of the sedan and walked around to hold Emily's door for her.

She joined him and they walked up the driveway to the front door. With every step they took, Mustang scanned the surrounding area, searching for anyone who might take a shot at Emily. He wished she hadn't insisted on coming along for the conversation with Jay Phillips. She would have been safer staying with Charlie at her estate with the other members of his team guarding her.

But then Mustang wouldn't have been able to keep his sights on her. He'd worry the entire time he was away. He trusted his team to protect her, but he felt more invested in her well-being and wanted to be the one looking out for her.

At the door, Emily pressed the doorbell.

Mustang could hear it echo in the interior of the structure.

After a full minute Emily pressed the button a second time. Again no one answered.

Emily glanced up at Mustang. "I hope the others had more luck at his office." She turned and took a step toward the car.

As Mustang turned with her, he heard a sound. He reached out to capture Emily's elbow, pulling her to a stop beside him. Then he pressed a finger to his lips and tilted his ear at the town house.

Another sound came from behind the door.

Mustang turned and banged on the door with his fist. "Mr. Phillips, we know you're in there. Open the door. We only want to talk to you."

No sounds emanated from inside the home.

Emily leaned closer to the door. "Mr. Phillips, it's me, Emily Chastain, the interpreter from our meeting with Ambassador Kozlov yesterday. I need to talk to you."

Nothing.

"Please, Mr. Phillips." She leaned her forehead against the door panel. "It's important. Someone is trying to kill me. I need your help."

Mustang couldn't let Emily stand out in the open any longer than necessary. He touched her shoulder and turned her toward the vehicle.

They'd just stepped off the porch when the door behind them opened.

Mustang spun and stepped in front of Emily.

A thin man with brown hair and brown eyes poked his head through the gap in the door. "Miss Chastain?"

Emily leaned around Mustang. "Yes. Mr. Phillips, are you okay?"

He shook his head, his gaze darting left then right. "Not really. I'm afraid to step out of my house."

"Has someone tried to attack you, as well?" Emily asked.

He nodded. "If I hadn't had such a good security system installed, I'd likely be a dead man by now." He frowned at Mustang. "Who's he?"

Emily gave the man a weak smile. "He's my bodyguard. I've been having a little trouble myself."

Mustang snorted. "Not just a little."

Phillips shot another glance around and opened the door a little wider. "You can come in."

Mustang followed Emily through the door and closed it.

Phillips reached around him, shot the dead bolt home and armed the security system through a panel on the wall.

"Come into the kitchen. It doesn't have any windows." Phillips led the way down the hall into a modern kitchen with granite countertops and dark cabinets. A small dinette table with four chairs took up a small corner. The private investigator nodded in that direction. "Have a seat and tell me you've had a better past twenty-four hours than I have."

Mustang held a chair for her and Emily sat.

"I can't say that my day's been better." She told him all that had happened in the last twenty-four hours, ending with the attack in the university parking garage.

Phillips ran a hand through his hair, making it stand on end. "Sounds like what I've experienced. I had an appointment across town from the Russian embassy after our meeting with Kozlov. I never made it there. Someone ran me off the road and down into a ditch. Fortunately, I was able to drive back out of it relatively unscathed. At least they let me go from the embassy. For a while, I wasn't sure they would. But I made up a story about my next appointment being with the military for an investigation on a base, and they'd be searching for me if I didn't show up. That seemed to tip them toward releasing me."

"You were luckier than I was. My car is totaled."

Phillips's lips twisted. "Yeah, but I spent the next couple of hours trying to lose the guy who'd run me off the road. I finally ended up hiding the night in a used car lot. I didn't sleep a wink. When I was pretty sure I wasn't going to be followed, I headed back here, only to find the alarm going off and the place surrounded by police." He smiled. "It was nice to know my security service worked. But once the police left, I haven't felt much like going out again. Not when someone is clearly trying to get to me."

"We've tried to call you," Emily interjected. "Mustang and his team."

"I hardly use my landline and let calls go to voice mail."

"Do you have any idea why someone would want to kill you two?" Mustang asked.

"I don't know. I've been trying to figure it out. Now that I know you're involved, it kind of narrows it down to the people and discussion that happened in the Russian embassy." He glanced toward Mustang. "We signed a nondisclosure agreement, but I'm seriously rethinking that at the moment."

"He knows pretty much what was discussed. Sachi Kozlov came to me, worried about her lover, Tyler Blunt, who went missing yesterday."

Phillips's eyes narrowed. "I heard that on the radio. Wow, who would think the ambassador would be angry enough to kill all those involved with his daughter's indiscretions?"

Emily shook her head. "It doesn't make sense."

"No. Something isn't right." Phillips ran his hand through his hair again, his mouth pinched in a tight line and the creases around his eyes deepening, making him appear older than his years. "Someone tried to break into my house."

"Do you have information they might not want shared? Information they might have tried to steal?" Mustang asked.

"Only the files I had on Blunt."

"You gave them the photos you'd taken," Emily said. "What more could they want?"

"I wasn't too worried about the images I left with the ambassador's assistant. Those were only the prints. I have digital copies of those photographs." He frowned.

"Do you suppose they were after the digital copies?"

"They would have to know how to get to them. I have them backed up to the cloud. Even if they got my desktop computer and laptop, they couldn't completely destroy them."

"What was in those pictures?" Mustang asked.

"I followed Blunt, capturing him and Sachi making clandestine assignations. I have photographs of them together outside restaurants and nightclubs."

Emily shrugged. "Again, it's not enough, in my mind, to want to kill us. We signed nondisclosures. We aren't going to the tabloids with the information."

"I'm not even sure they'd care who Sachi is going out with," Mustang said. "It's not like she's the First Daughter or a celebrity."

"True," Phillips said. "I'll go back through those photographs, in case I missed something important."

"Could you forward them to me?" Emily asked. "It might help to have a second set of eyes reviewing them."

Phillips shook his head. "Not yet."

Emily nodded. "I know. The nondisclosure agreement." She empathized, "I wouldn't want you to compromise your integrity."

"But you'd think all bets were off when someone is trying to kill you." Mustang held up his hand. "I understand. It's your word. A person's word is gold."

"And it's my livelihood. If people found out I don't hold true to my promise of complete discretion, I wouldn't have a business."

"You won't have a life if we don't figure this out soon," Mustang said, clearly trying to press the man into disclosing more.

"I get that. I just want to review the photos first and decide what to do. I promise you'll be hearing from me if something turns up. But I'm not handing over every single snapshot. Not yet anyway."

Emily leaned across the table and touched the man's arm. "Will you be all right?"

He shrugged. "I have my security system and enough food in my refrigerator and pantry to last a week." Phillips gave Emily half a smile. "Surely they'll give up after that."

"If you need anything, we can bring it. All you have to do is call." Emily dug in her purse and handed Phillips one of her business cards.

"Got a pen?" Mustang held out his hand.

Emily pulled a pen out of her purse and handed it to him.

Mustang scribbled his and Declan's cell phone numbers on the back of Emily's card. "Call either one of those numbers. We can help."

"Thank you," Phillips said, his shoulders sagging. "I've been in the PI business for twenty years, but I've never been this close to being killed. I pride myself in blending in. But no amount of blending seems to work in this situation. I'll have a look at my images again. I'll let you know if I find anything unusual."

Emily squeezed Phillips's arm. "Thank you. And please, stay safe."

The private investigator narrowed his eyes. "Same goes for you," he said. "I can see someone coming after me, but it doesn't make any sense that they would come after the interpreter."

"I couldn't agree with you more." Mustang stood and touched Emily's arm. "I'd like to get back to the estate before dark."

"Let's make that stop at the organization that hired me to translate. She nodded and pushed to her feet. "Then I'm ready to head back to the estate."

"I'll be in touch, one way or another," Phillips promised. He pulled his own card out of his pocket and handed it over. "This has my private cell on it that I don't give out to everyone."

"Thank you," Emily said.

Mustang held out his hand.

Phillips took it and shook with a surprisingly strong grip. "Prior military?" he asked.

Mustang nodded. "Marines."

Phillips's shoulders squared and his grip tightened on Mustang's hand. "Semper Fi."

"Semper Fi," Mustang echoed. "Stay safe."

Mustang led the way to the door and exited first, performing a swift evaluation of the street, houses and bushes nearby. A car slowed as it approached.

When Emily moved to step out onto the porch, Mustang's arm shot out, stopping her in a clothesline move—straight arm across her chest.

Her eyes widened. "What's wrong?"

The vehicle slid by at a slow pace and Mustang could peer into the interior.

An old man hunched over the wheel, as if struggling to see the road in front of him.

"Nothing. It was just an old man."

She smiled up at him. "Getting punchy?"

He nodded. "After being shot at in the university parking garage, I'm thinking punchy is a good way to be while we're out and about."

Emily shivered. "You're right. She touched his arm, sending a shock of awareness through his body. "You go right on being punchy. I'd rather be safe than sorry."

Her hand slid down his arm to capture his fingers with hers. For a moment he held her hand, enjoying the coolness of her fingertips against his warm palm. Then he released her fingers and wrapped his arm around her shoulders and walked with her to the car.

Once she was safely inside, he got in, shifted into Reverse and pulled out of the driveway onto the street.

They made a quick stop at the office that hired her for the translation. The administrative staff had nothing to add that would help them in their investigation.

It was early afternoon and traffic was just picking up. People from all over the city rushed to get home, causing the roads to clog and vehicles to move at a snail's pace. By the time they reached the Halverson estate, dusk was creeping up on the trees, casting long, dark shadows over the landscape.

Mustang pulled up to the gate and pointed at a section of the stone wall. "They already have the wall back up."

Emily shook her head. "That's amazing."

"I guess when you have as much money as Charlie Halverson, things get done a heck of a lot quicker."

"She seems like such a strong woman, yet she surrounds herself with the best in security systems and personnel."

"For a reason," Mustang said. "Her husband was killed and there was an attempt on her own life. That's how she met Declan. A group of men took her from her limousine in a kidnapping attempt. If Declan had not been there when he was, she could be dead."

"Grace told me about what happened. It's a miracle he got her out alive."

"Right place, right time."

"Right hero." Emily smiled in his direction.

"Declan will be the first to tell you he isn't a hero. Our team has been operating on the rule of *if you see something that needs doing, you do it.* It's purely reflex."

"Hero reflexes," Emily insisted. "And save your breath. You won't convince me otherwise." She laid a hand on his leg and squeezed lightly.

Before she could remove the hand, Mustang pressed his over hers. "Just promise me you won't tell Declan he's a hero. It would go to his head and he'd be impossible to live with." Mustang gave her a sly grin.

Emily held up her free hand. "I promise."

Mustang maneuvered along the driveway to the big house with one hand on the steering wheel, the other still holding Emily's. He didn't want to let go.

All the way, he kept a watchful eye on the shadows beneath the surrounding trees. Charlie would have beefed up the security, but whoever was after Emily had breached the estate's protection once. He could do it again.

Chapter Twelve

Emily couldn't remember a time when she was more exhausted. The stress of being on guard all day had taken its toll. The only thing holding her up from collapse was Mustang's arm around her as she stood in the foyer, a frown marring her brow, as Charlie greeted her. "I heard what happened at the university." She gripped Emily's hands in hers. "Are you all right?"

Emily nodded. "I am." She turned to Mustang. "We both are."

Charlie's gaze went to Mustang. "Thank God you were there to get her out alive." She hooked her arm through Emily's. "Come. You must be starving. I want to hear all about your visit to Mr. Phillips. Did you learn anything new?"

Charlie led Emily and Mustang into the kitchen and urged them to sit at the large table while she worked with her chef to deliver a substantial meal for the two of them.

"Aren't you going to eat, too?" Emily asked.

"We finished dinner less than an hour ago. We saved plates for you and Mustang. Will chicken cordon bleu be enough for you?" She placed meals in front of both of them.

"More than enough," Emily said, her stomach rumbling as she sniffed the heavenly scent of roasted chicken wrapped around ham and cheese with a delicate layer of breading. Her mouth watered as she cut off a piece and brought it to her lips.

Heaven. Pure heaven.

She moaned her pleasure.

Beside her, Mustang chuckled. "I don't think I've ever seen anyone eat a bite of chicken with quite that much enthusiasm."

Heat rose in Emily's cheeks. She cut off another slice of the chicken. "We didn't have lunch, did we?"

Mustang shook his head. "We were otherwise occupied staying alive." He took a bite of the chicken, too, and nodded. "This really is good." He nodded to the chef, busy preparing the kitchen for the next day's meals. "My compliments to the chef. Sure beats MREs."

Emily frowned. "MREs?"

"Meals ready to eat," Mustang said. "The

prepackaged stuff they feed the troops in the field." He leaned back, his brow rising. "You've never had MREs?"

Emily shook her head. "Never."

"Sweetheart, we have to improve your education. You need to try them so that you'll know just how good this chicken is."

"I know how good it is," Emily said and glanced down at her empty plate. "I don't think I actually took a breath between bites."

Charlie laughed. "Carl, my chef, can make a can of Spam taste like a culinary masterpiece." She gave the chef a chin lift. "Isn't that right, Carl?"

"Yes, ma'am," he answered.

"Carl is prior navy. He was a chef on board the USS *La Salle*." Charlie smiled. "My husband knew the ship's captain. When Carl left active duty, the captain asked him if he had a place for him in one of our businesses." Charlie's lips quirked. "John saw his potential, sent him to culinary school and he went to work for us as our personal chef."

"I love it almost as much as I loved cooking for the navy," Carl called out.

Charlie snorted. "I know I'll lose him someday to some fancy restaurant, but I'm enjoying some really good meals in the meantime."

She sighed heavily. "So, tell me what happened today."

Emily recounted Sachi's visit, the attack in the parking garage and their visit with Jay Phillips. "I'm sad to report, we're no closer to learning who my attacker is."

"But we do know more than we started out with," Mustang added. "Whoever is after Emily is also after Phillips. Which must have something to do with what was discussed at the meeting with the ambassador."

"And since Sachi spilled the beans about why her father contracted the private investigator in the first place," Emily said, "I can speak freely about the meeting with the PI and the ambassador without violating my nondisclosure agreement."

"Good." Charlie clapped her hands together. "At least there's that. We haven't had much luck here. Cole McCastlain and Jonah Spradlin, my computer guy, have been online all morning, trying to find the dirt on the Russians occupying the embassy. So far, other than being accused of employing an undocumented maid at one of the Russian's town homes, we haven't uncovered anything of significance that would warrant someone wanting you and Mr. Phillips dead."

Emily laid her napkin on the table. "I don't

know what else I can do, other than go back to the embassy and ask for a meeting with the ambassador himself." She shrugged. "I'm not sure what good that will do, other than to let him know one of two things. Either I'm on to his attempts on my life or he's got a problem with someone on his staff who feels it necessary to keep his daughter's love affair quiet from the rest of the world."

Mustang shook his head. "I still find it hard to believe a daughter's indiscretions would create enough of a stir to warrant an attack on an interpreter and a PI."

Emily frowned. "Unless it goes back to the fact I saw Tyler Blunt at the embassy the day he disappeared. Do you think that's the crux of the matter? Have the Russians done something nefarious with Tyler?"

"I can have some of Declan's Defenders follow the ambassador," Charlie offered.

"It wouldn't hurt," Mustang said.

"While you're at it, have Viktor Sokolov, the ambassador's assistant, followed," Emily said. "He was at the meeting, as well, along with a couple of their embassy guards. I'm sorry, I didn't get their names."

Charlie tapped her chin with the tip of her finger. "I doubt they would be pulling the strings on your attackers."

Mustang frowned. "If anything, they might be the ones attacking you."

"All I know is I need a shower." She yawned, covering her mouth. "I might call it a night early."

"I'm sure you're exhausted," Charlie said.

Emily gave the older woman a crooked smile. "At least I was able to collect some of my own belongings." She glanced around, looking for the bag she'd packed. "I must have left my things in the car."

Charlie held up a hand. "I had Arnold take your bag to your room. You go on up. I'll have Carl make you a cup of tea and send it up."

"That's not necessary," Emily said. "I can come down and get it myself."

"Please. I insist." Charlie pressed her lips together. "I like having the company. I just wish the circumstances weren't so dire."

Emily pushed back from the table and stood.

Mustang rose with her and cupped her elbow.

"You don't have to go with me," Emily said. "I can find my way."

With a shake of his head, Mustang didn't slow as he ushered her from the dining room. "I told you, I'm sticking with you. I don't want you out of my sight for more than a couple of seconds."

Emily opened her mouth to argue but ended

up saying, "Thank you." Nothing she could say or do would put Mustang at ease. Until her attacker was stopped, she'd have the former marine as her shadow. After all that had happened, she was glad he was there.

As Charlie had indicated, Emily's bag had been brought to her room and deposited on the bed. Thankful for her own clothes, she dug into the garments and selected clean underwear and hesitated over what to sleep in.

She ran her hand over her usual nightgown, though she wondered what Mustang would think of her in it. The gown was a sexy, blush pink babydoll that barely covered her bottom, with matching pink panties. Why she'd tossed it into the bag, she didn't know. Mustang would be sleeping in her bedroom until further notice. The gown was too revealing to wear in the presence of the marine. He might think she was coming on to him.

Her pulse quickened and warmth pooled low in her belly at the thought of standing in front of Mustang in a nightie that didn't conceal much beneath the shear fabric. She shot a glance in his direction.

Mustang had closed and secured the bedroom door before wandering through the room and bathroom. He ended up in front of the French doors leading out onto the balcony.

Having pulled the curtain aside, he stared out at the night. The man obviously wasn't interested in seeing her in a nightgown. She'd practically had to beg him to sleep with her the night before, to chase away the lingering shadows of her nightmare. The man was in her room out of necessity not desire.

Emily grabbed a pair of dark leggings and a long-sleeved T-shirt and headed for the shower, closing the bathroom door behind her. She'd stripped out of her clothes and turned on the shower before she realized she'd left her bag of toiletries on the bed.

Wrapping one of the huge, plush towels around her, Emily opened the door and poked her head out.

Mustang stood directly in front of her, only inches away, with one fist raised to knock, the other hand holding her toiletries bag. "Forget this?"

Her eyes widened and heat rushed up her neck into her cheeks. Even more heat raced south to the juncture of her naked thighs beneath the towel. "Uh, yes." When she reached for the bag, her towel slipped. She held it up with one hand and tried again to take the bag.

The corners of Mustang's lips quirked as he handed over the item.

When his fingers touched hers, Emily felt a

jolt of something like electricity shoot up her arm and across her chest, making her nipples tighten and her breath catch in her lungs. Her eyes widened as she held the bag he hadn't released yet.

For a long moment she stared into his eyes.

And he stared back.

Finally he let go and backed away, jabbing a thumb over his shoulder. "I'm just going to wait in the adjoining room, but I'll leave the door open." Then he turned and strode into the other room. He paused at the connecting door and glanced back over his shoulder.

Emily stood for a moment longer, unable to draw in a breath. Wow. What had just happened?

He ducked around the corner and the moment was gone.

Clutching the bag to her chest, Emily slipped back into the bathroom and closed the door. Then she turned and leaned against it and tried to remember how to breathe. The man turned her inside out and made her heart flutter. No man had ever done that. Why Mustang? And, for heaven's sake, why now?

MUSTANG PACED THE floor of his bedroom, passing the open connecting door several times before he slowed to a stop and stood staring across Emily's room to the closed bathroom door.

When she'd poked her head out, wearing nothing but a towel, all thoughts of keeping her at arm's length flew out the window. He'd wanted to take her into his arms and hold her naked body against his. Hell, he wanted to do more than that. His gaze drifted to the bed and he groaned. How the heck was he going to keep this mission from becoming too personal? With all that was going on, Emily didn't need a lusty former marine panting after her.

He closed his eyes and willed his body to calm down. But the image that resonated in his mind was one of her creamy shoulders above the terry-cloth towel and her long, sexy legs that would wrap so easily around his waist.

Mustang opened his eyes and forced himself to look at anything but the bed and the bathroom door. He turned into his room and stared at the go-bag he'd carried on more missions than he cared to remember. Perhaps it was time to pack it again and let one of the other team members take on the responsibility of keeping Emily safe and alive.

As soon as the thought entered his head, he pushed it back. No. As much as he trusted his team to support him and to do a good job at any tasking, Mustang couldn't walk away. Emily was his.

He ran a hand through his hair.

Correction... Emily wasn't his. Keeping her alive was his mission. He would not fail. That meant he would not let her out of his sight. He couldn't let someone else provide her protection. He'd just have to manage his baser instincts and do his best not to touch her any more than he had to.

Just as he was coming to that conclusion, the bathroom door opened and Emily stepped out, wearing leggings and a long-sleeved shirt. All the drool-worthy parts of her body were covered and her hair was wet and combed straight back. The sloppy outfit and wet hair didn't make her any less sexy. If anything, the tips of her nipples making little tents against her shirt were more of a tease than exposed flesh.

Another groan rose up his throat and would have escaped if Emily's cell phone hadn't buzzed at that exact moment.

Mustang swallowed hard and hurried forward.

Emily lifted the phone from the bed and frowned down at the display.

Mustang leaned over her shoulder and read the text message.

I might have something. Meet me at Finnegan's Tavern in Arlington in thirty minutes. JP.

"I can be dressed in one minute. Do we have time to make it to Finnegan's in thirty minutes?" Emily grabbed a bra from her suitcase and tucked it beneath her T-shirt, reaching to clasp it in the back. Then she pulled her arms out of the sleeves and into the torso of the shirt. After a few moments of fumbling beneath the fabric, she pushed her arms back through the sleeves and gave him a twisted grin. "You could have turned your back."

"Yeah, sorry. I've always been intrigued at how dexterous a woman can be when dressing."

Emily grabbed a pair of shoes and slipped her feet into them. "I'm ready."

"I'm not sure you should go," Mustang said. "I need to run this by Declan and the team."

"He texted me. He'll be expecting me." Her lips firmed. "I'm going."

"What if it wasn't him who texted? What if it's a setup?"

She grabbed her phone as he stepped closer, calling Phillips.

"Voice mail," she said and hit End.

"See? Might not have been him."

"Or he might be on the road." She stared at him. "I'm going. Like it or not, I'm going."

"Okay. But we do it my way. And we need backup." He led the way down the stairs and into the living area where he found Declan, Grace, Charlie and Charlie's computer guy, Jonah Spradlin. "We just got word from Phillips. He wants to meet in twenty-five minutes. Finnegan's in Arlington. He thinks he has something."

Declan leaned over and kissed Grace. "Snow and I are with you. Mack and Gus are on their way home. We can divert them to the location."

"He texted me," Emily reminded them. "He'll be expecting me, and Mustang. But he might spook if the whole gang of us shows up."

Declan nodded. "Understood. We won't all enter at the same time. In fact, I can position a couple guys outside the tavern to be on the lookout for trouble."

Mustang glanced down at the clock on his cell phone. "We'd better get moving." Whatever Phillips had could be the break they were looking for. They couldn't blow it by being late.

The garage doors were up and the sedan Mustang and Emily had arrived in was pulling out as Mustang, Emily, Declan and Snow emerged from the back door of the big house.

Arnold climbed out, left the driver's door

open and then ran around to the other side and opened the door for Emily.

Emily and Mustang slid in and buckled their seat belts.

"I'll have the gate open as you reach it," Arnold promised.

"Thanks," Mustang called out as he shifted into Drive and sped away from the garage.

Declan and Snow climbed into Declan's truck and pulled in behind them.

By the time they reached the gate it was three-quarters of the way open, just enough for him to squeeze the sedan through. Emily had the address of the tavern keyed into the map on her phone. They were on the road to their rendezvous with little time to spare.

With Declan's headlights in the rearview mirror, Mustang felt marginally better about the meeting. He couldn't keep watch in all directions, and the attackers had showed some ability to create a distraction. Having the rest of the team there would make it easier to keep Emily safe.

Pushing the speed limits, Mustang wove through the city, from main roads to those with less traffic, arriving with two minutes to spare.

When Emily reached for the door handle, Mustang shot out a hand to capture her arm.

"I'm still not comfortable with you going in. It smells like a setup to me."

Emily let go of the handle as if it burned her hand. "But why would Jay go along with a setup?"

"He might not be in control of his cell phone." He pulled his own phone out of his pocket and punched the key for Declan.

"I'm going in first," Declan answered without preamble.

Mustang chuckled. "You read my mind. We'll wait for your signal."

Declan had parked his truck out of sight of the tavern's front door and approached the building, using the sidewalk, like any other customer intent on a meal or a pint.

Once Declan entered, Mustang gave him a minute or two to get settled and then he gave Emily's arm a gentle squeeze. "Stay low until I get out and come around."

Emily did as he told her, waiting for him to open her door and usher her out of the vehicle. Once again, using his body as a shield, he guided her into the tavern, certain Declan would have made sure it was relatively safe. If it hadn't been, he'd have found a way to notify Mustang before he dared enter with Emily.

Once inside, Mustang scanned the interior. At that moment he wished he had his military rifle and bulletproof body armor on both him and Emily. He didn't know what to expect, but his gut was telling him to count on trouble. For a moment he considered turning around and marching Emily out, high-tailing it back to the Halverson estate.

Then he spotted Declan who gave him an almost imperceptive chin lift. A further study of the interior of the tavern revealed a lack of Jay Phillips.

Emily craned her neck, frowning. "I don't see him."

"He said he'd meet us here in a half hour. We're right on time, he might have gotten tied up in traffic," Mustang reasoned. "Give him a few minutes."

Emily nodded. "You're right. I'm just nervous. I really hope he's come up with something that would give us a clue as to who is targeting us."

Mustang guided her to a table in a corner and took the seat that placed him with his back against the wall. It also gave him a view of the front entrance and the rear exit.

Rather than sitting across the table from Mustang, Emily chose to sit in the seat beside him, giving her a good view of the entrance.

The waitress came and handed them two

dinner menus and a drinks menu. "Can I get you a drink to start with?"

"I'll have coffee," Mustang said, anxious for the woman to move and quit blocking his view of the doors.

"Hot tea for me," Emily said softly.

"I'll be back with your drinks and to take your dinner order."

Mustang didn't bother to tell the waitress they weren't interested in eating. He just wanted her to move on.

Emily lifted her napkin and laid it across her lap, her fingers pulling at the hem, her gaze worried and turned to the entrance.

With a chuckle, Mustang covered her hand with his. "You'd be a terrible secret agent," he said.

She frowned. "Why do you say that?"

"You're wearing your emotions on your face. Anyone looking at you would know you're waiting for someone to enter. Someone you're nervous about meeting or seeing."

Her frown deepened. "How am I wearing my emotions on my face?"

Mustang reached out and brushed his thumb across her brow. "You're frowning fiercely. Why don't you pretend we are here on a date? Not the kind of date where you're about to dump me."

Emily lifted a hand halfway to her face and then let it drop to her lap. "You're right. I'm worried, and I'm sure it shows." She pasted a smile on her face. "There, is that better?"

He winced and gave her a crooked smile. "A little, but a bit scary." He winked and gave her a natural smile. What wasn't to smile about? She was a beautiful woman and they were alone at the table together.

She sighed. "You make it look so natural and easy."

"I think of something besides why we're here. A more pleasant reason to be sitting here with you. Like if we were on a real date." He reached out and took her hand in his and wove her fingers through his. Though he gazed into her eyes, he kept a close watch in his peripheral vision on the doors.

Emily's fingers curled around his. "I wish we were here for that reason. Not because we need information on my attacker. I'd order a glass of wine and stare across the table into your eyes, not frantically watch the door for another man to enter."

He gently squeezed her hand. "Sounds good to me. Maybe when this is all over, we can do that." Out of the corner of his eye, he spotted a man fitting Jay Phillips's build slipping through the front door. He wore a sweatshirt with a hood pulled up over his head.

As soon as he spotted Emily, the man pushed the hood away from his face and hurried toward them.

"Phillips is here," Mustang announced softly.

Chapter Thirteen

Emily's fingers tightened around Mustang's and she turned toward the investigator.

The man hurried across the bar and sat in the chair opposite Mustang. "I think I was followed," he said and glanced over his shoulder.

Mustang leaned toward Phillips and spoke softly. "We have a couple guys here as backup."

Phillips shook his head. "I should have stayed home. By leaving, I might as well have painted a target on my back."

Emily placed her hand on the man's arm. "Tell us what you came to say. We'll make sure you get out of here safely, won't we?" Her gaze met Mustang's.

He nodded. "We will. But you have to trust me and my team."

"They've been watching me. I had to create a diversion in order for me to get out of my house without being seen. I called the police to my neighbor's house, saying I thought someone was trying to break in. When a couple cruisers arrived, I slipped out the back door of my house and escaped on my motorcycle."

Emily tightened her hold on the private investigator's arm. "Jay, what did you come here to say?"

He pulled a small electronic tablet from a backpack he'd worn over his hoodie. Pressing the on switch, he glanced around and then leaned closer to Emily. "I found something in one of the most recent photographs I took of the ambassador's daughter and the journalist. They were leaving the restaurant at one of the hotels in Alexandria. I snapped the photo as they passed an alley."

As the photo materialized on the screen, Emily leaned in. Though the image was a bit blurry, Emily recognized Sachi Kozlov and Tyler Blunt. They were holding hands as they walked by the alley. "So, we know they were seeing each other. Why is this image so important?"

Phillips touched the screen, enlarging the image. He pointed to the alley behind the couple. "Do you see the people in the background?"

Emily squinted, concentrating on the dimly lit space behind the couple. "A little. There's a man and a woman."

"Look closer." The PI enlarged the image yet again, making it even grainier.

"The man looks familiar, but I can't quite place him."

Phillips pulled the tablet back and thumbed the touch screen until another image popped into view.

Emily's heartbeat kicked up a notch. "The ambassador's assistant, Viktor Sokolov." She glanced up at the PI. "You think the man in the alley is Sokolov?"

Phillips touched the screen and brought up both images side by side.

Emily compared the two, her eyes growing wider. "Looks like him. But who is the woman with him?"

"I don't know, but she looks really young."

Mustang studied the image. "Too young."

"She can't be more than fourteen."

"It's hard to tell by a picture," Phillips admitted. "But she doesn't look happy about being with him. And they're waiting at a door to the back of the hotel."

A chill rippled down the back of Emily's neck. "You think Sokolov is having an affair with a minor? Is that what this is all about?"

Phillips ran a hand through his hair. "I don't know, but what are the chances Blunt and Sokolov happen to be at the same hotel at the same time?"

"Blunt is an investigative reporter. Could he have been probing Sokolov's activities?" Mustang asked.

"We can't know until someone has the opportunity to ask Blunt," Phillips said.

"And you think someone at the embassy has kidnapped Blunt because of what he might know about Sokolov's activities?" Emily asked.

Phillips nodded. "I looked through all of my photos of Blunt and the ambassador's daughter and this is the only one that stood out. Why else would they be after me?"

"And I saw Blunt at the embassy. I know the ambassador was angry about his daughter going out with the journalist, but I can't imagine it being enough to make him want to kidnap or kill the man."

Phillips frowned. "Unless he's in on whatever Sokolov is doing. Either way, this photograph could be what has them spooked and willing to come after me."

"You have the photos backed up in case someone destroys your equipment and computer storage device, right?" Mustang asked.

Phillips nodded. "Yeah, on the cloud. Only I know how to get to them."

"The Russians have been known to be good at hacking," Mustang reminded Phillips.

"That's why I wanted to meet in person. I was afraid if I sent it, with an explanation, it could somehow get diverted into the wrong hands. I've saved them in multiple places. It will take them time to hack into my account. And even more time to hack into multiple accounts."

"Could you send me a copy of that photo now? Our system is secure," Mustang said. "I have people who can do some sleuthing on this Sokolov guy and see what they can come up with."

Mustang gave him the email address to Cole McCastlain.

After a few clicks on the tablet, Phillips looked up. "Sent." He looked again at the front entrance. "Now, I need to go before they catch up with me." Phillips rose from his seat.

Emily rose with him. "Will you be all right?"

Phillips pressed his lips together in a tight line. "Only time will tell."

Mustang held out his hand. "Thanks for bringing this to us at a risk to your own life."

"I wanted someone else to know what I'd found. It wouldn't do anyone any good if I was knocked off before the images could be reviewed even closer."

"Thank you." Mustang held out his hand. "And please, let us help you get somewhere safe. We could put you up for a while, until this blows over."

"Thanks, but I'm going to get out of town." He started toward the entrance.

Before Phillips had taken three steps, Declan launched himself out of his seat and tackled Phillips.

At that moment a loud crash sounded and a vehicle erupted into the tavern, smashing through one of the walls and rolling to a stop mere inches from where Declan lay on top of Phillips.

The crash made Emily rock back on her heels and fall into the seat she'd just vacated.

Declan jumped to his feet, pulled his gun and aimed it at the crashed vehicle.

With the weight lifted from his body, Phillips leaped to his feet and ran for the rear exit.

"Jay!" Emily called out. "It could be a trap!"

But the man was gone, through the back door and out into the night.

"Go after him!" Emily said.

"I won't leave you," Mustang said.

"Fine, then follow me." She ran toward the back door.

Mustang followed close behind. "Don't go out there," he called out.

Just as Emily reached the back door, she heard the sound of an engine starting and then the squeal of tires on the pavement outside the crumbled tavern.

By the time she opened the door and peered out, Phillips was speeding away on his motorcycle.

"Come on." Mustang stepped past her into the night then pulled her into the crook of his arm and ran for the other side of the building where he'd parked the car. "If we hurry, we can catch up to him and maybe make sure he gets away safely."

Emily picked up the pace, running as fast as she could.

They reached the sedan in seconds, climbed in and raced off in the direction Phillips had gone.

Mustang tossed his cell phone to Emily. "Call Declan and let him know where we're going."

Emily fumbled with the device and brought up the contacts list. "Where are we going?"

"After Phillips," Mustang said. He rounded the corner and hit the accelerator, making the sedan leap forward.

Ahead, several blocks away, a bright red taillight glowed on a motorcycle.

"There he is," Mustang murmured, his focus

on the vehicle ahead as Emily clicked on the number for Mustang's leader.

Declan answered on the first ring. "Mack and I will catch up to you," he said, without waiting for Emily to fill him in on where they were going. "Just give us a street name and direction."

Emily frantically looked for a street sign and then passed on the information he needed.

"Thanks. We'll be with you as soon as possible," Declan said.

"What happened back there?" Emily asked.

"Another diversion," Declan said. "These people don't believe in being subtle. But don't worry, we'll have your back."

Emily ended the call and concentrated on keeping track of the motorcycle ahead of them. "Are we trying to stop him?" she asked.

"No. I just want to make sure he gets far enough away before someone catches up to him and makes another attempt on his life," Mustang said.

As if conjured by Mustang's words, a van pulled out of a side street ahead and slammed into the motorcycle Phillips was riding.

Phillips flew into the air and landed several yards away, skidding to a stop on the pavement.

"Oh my God," Emily whispered, the horror

of the scene making her stomach roil and her hands shake.

Mustang punched his foot harder on the accelerator, speeding toward the downed PI as the vehicle that hit him backed up, dragging the motorcycle beneath its chassis. It bumped up over the mangled wreckage and shifted forward, heading for the man on the ground.

Emily leaned toward the windshield. "Hurry, Mustang! You can't let him run over Jay."

Mustang raced ahead, coming up on the left side of the van. He turned his wheel sharply to the right, making the car hit the van hard on the right rear bumper.

The van spun around, performing a one-hundred-and-eighty-degree turn until it faced the little sedan Mustang and Emily were in.

Emily leaned back in her seat and braced herself. "He's going to hit us—"

The van plowed into them, clipping the front driver's-side bumper, sending them spinning toward the curb and a solid light pole.

At the last moment Mustang swung the steering wheel around. The little sedan crashed into an abandoned warehouse, where part of the old walls came crumbling down around them.

The airbags deployed, slamming Emily back into her seat. No sooner had they exploded in

her face than the bags deflated, leaving Emily
stunned and powder-coated.

"Get out!" Mustang ordered from beside her.
"Get out now!" He pushed his door open, shoving aside rubble to exit.

Emily tried to do the same but couldn't get
her door to budge. She unbuckled her seat belt
and crawled across the console, escaping out
the driver's side.

"What about Jay?" she said, looking back.

A shot rang out nearby.

"The team will help him." Mustang grabbed
her hand and took off running through the dark
building where their vehicle had landed, with
nothing but the dull glow of exterior streetlights shining through windows high up on the
walls guiding them.

Emily had no other choice but to follow or
have her arm yanked out of its socket. She ran,
trying her best to keep up with Mustang's longer stride, dodging abandoned crates and pallets.

In the shadowy expanse, Emily could just
make out a row of doors. She had no idea
where they led or if they would be locked when
they got there. But the sound of several pairs of
footsteps pounding behind her kept her moving forward, praying one of the doors opened

to the outside where they might have a chance to escape.

Another shot rang out, the sound closer and louder, as if it had been fired from right behind them.

Emily ducked automatically but didn't slow. She pushed harder, running as fast as she could, her lungs burning and her pulse pounding so loudly against her eardrums she could barely hear herself think.

Mustang reached the doors and tried the first one. It opened.

He ran inside, pulling Emily in behind him.

The darkness was complete behind the door.

Emily swept her finger across Mustang's cell phone that she still held in her hand and turned on the flashlight application. The little light illuminated the space enough to let them see they'd ended up in a stairwell where the only way to go was up.

Mustang took the steps two at a time, until he realized Emily couldn't keep up.

She tried, but her legs just weren't as long and strong and she was already struggling for breath, having run the length of what felt like a football field inside the warehouse. But she couldn't stop.

The sound of the door opening at ground level and clanking shut made her climb faster.

When they reached the top of the stairs, Mustang shoved open the door and led her into a long hallway with a door leading off to either side.

"Which one?" Emily whispered.

Mustang tried the first. It was locked. The second and third weren't, but he kept moving, trying the doors as he went.

A little over halfway down the hall, he ducked into a door on the right and yanked Emily inside. As he pulled the door closed behind them, the door to the stairwell clanked open at the end of the hallway.

Emily clamped a hand over her mouth to keep from gasping.

Mustang started to twist the lock on the door and stopped.

"Why aren't you locking it?"

"They might think we're in here, if we engage the lock. We need to hide. I'd fight them, but I'm not sure just how many there are. I think I heard three sets of footsteps, but I can't be sure."

Emily shone the cell phone light around the room, locating another door, a modular metal desk, a giant metal cabinet and a large credenza.

Mustang ran for the other door and pushed it open. He shook his head and retreated into the room with Emily. "No good. Only another desk, not big enough for both of us to fit beneath."

Emily pointed to the credenza. "I can fit in that," she offered and started toward it.

Mustang shook his head and pointed to the modular desk. "Get under that," he urged quietly.

Footsteps sounded in the hallway, along with deep, male voices.

Emily dove behind the desk.

Mustang followed, pressing his body against hers, pushing her as far forward as they could both be and still be hidden behind the metal skirting around the front of the office furniture. "Douse the light."

Emily fumbled with the phone and managed to turn off the flashlight.

The sound of doors opening and closing grew closer and faster as more than one man searched the floor for them.

A metal click echoed, as if the doorknob to the room in which they hid had been turned. Footsteps sounded, moving toward the desk.

Emily held her breath.

Behind her Mustang rolled over, placing his back against hers, his body tense, ready to spring should the intruder round the desk and look beneath.

The footsteps seemed to lead away from the desk and toward the other doors. One clicked open and shut pretty quickly. He must have found the broom closet they'd passed and Mustang had rejected as a hiding place. Then the other door clicked open and the steps sounded as if they were going away.

A moment later they were back and stopped in front of the massive desk.

Something thumped softly against the floor.

A voice called out in Russian from the hallway, "Did you find them?"

The man standing in front of the desk responded, "*Nyet.*"

"Someone is coming. We must leave."

Emily waited, willing the man on the other side of the desk to go and leave them alone.

Finally he did, his steps leading away from them and out the door to echo in the hallway with the others. Moments later the hallway was silent.

Emily didn't move. Neither did Mustang. After what felt like an eternity, which was probably only a minute, maybe two, Mustang rolled from beneath the desk and held out his hand to Emily.

She grasped it and let him pull her to her feet and into his arms.

He held her for a long time, his arms like

steel bands around her middle, reassuring in their strength.

Emily slipped her arms around his neck and looked up into his eyes. "That was…"

She didn't get the chance to finish her sentence.

Mustang's mouth came down on hers, crushing her lips in a kiss that left her knees weak and her heart hammering.

He traced the seam of her lips with his tongue.

When she opened to him, he swept in and claimed her, deepening the kiss until she couldn't think past his mouth on hers.

When he finally lifted his head, he stared down at her. "I know the timing isn't great, but I've wanted to do that since I first kissed you."

She smiled at him and then leaned up on her toes and pressed her lips to his. "I wanted you to, ever since you saved me from being shot."

He took her again, slowly this time, gathering her closer.

Emily could have stayed in his arms forever, but an incessant ringing sounded, pulling her back to reality.

She glanced down at the phone still in her hand. It was dark and silent.

Emily and Mustang glanced around the room

and finally located the ringing sound coming from another cell phone lying on the floor.

A second later they heard the sound of footsteps pounding down the hallway toward them.

Mustang grabbed her hand and yanked her into the broom closet inside the office. He managed to pull the door almost all the way closed without clicking the lever, as the outer office door burst open.

Emily stood in the circle of Mustang's arms, her pulse pounding and her breath lodged in her throat.

Through the gap, she could see the shadow of a man leaning over to grab up the cell phone that was still ringing. He hit the answer key and turned to leave.

Something shifted behind Emily. A broom or a mop, she didn't know. But it made just enough noise to alert the man in the other room.

He spun toward the door they were hiding behind. Still holding the phone to his ear, he paused.

A shout sounded in the hallway.

The man pocketed his phone, pivoted on his heel and raced out the door.

A distant voice called out, muffled by walls and doors. It sounded like someone yelling, "Mustang! Emily!"

Mustang's hands gripped her arms and his head lowered in the darkness until his lips found hers. "We need to talk. Later. Right now, I need you to stay here. I have to warn Declan in case those thugs are still hanging around. I'll be back when I'm sure the coast is clear." He dropped a kiss on her mouth and then stepped out of the closet.

"Mustang." Emily reached a hand out and grabbed Mustang's arm.

He took her hand in his and raised it to his lips.

If anything happened to him… Emily swallowed hard on the lump in her throat. "Be careful," she whispered.

Chapter Fourteen

Mustang peeked out the door of the office and checked the hallway. It was empty. He held his gun in front of him as he eased out into the hall.

"Mustang! Emily!" Declan's voice called out, this time a little more clearly but muffled by walls.

Mustang thought he'd heard the man who'd been in the office with them run off to the right. Declan's call came from the direction of the stairwell. He glanced in both directions. If he went after the people who'd been looking for him and Emily, he'd leave her exposed. They might return and find her hiding in the broom closet.

Instead of racing after the bad guys, Mustang hunkered low to the floor and held his handgun pointed at the opposite end of the hallway from where Declan would emerge. He'd provide cover for his team as they entered into the hallway and remain close enough to Emily to keep her safe.

As he suspected, Declan emerged from the stairwell a few seconds later. He dove into the hallway, rolled to his feet and came up aiming his weapon at Mustang.

Mustang raised a hand and spoke in a low tone that wouldn't carry any farther than his team leader. "It's me. But there were others here right before you arrived."

Mack and Snow emerged behind Declan and the three of them joined Mustang in front of the office, holding their aim on the other end of the hall.

Declan glanced over Mustang's shoulder. "Where's Emily? Is she all right?"

Mustang nodded. "She's hiding in there. I don't want her to come out until I know for sure someone isn't going to shoot at her."

"Good. Stay here. We'll clear the building." Declan started forward.

"With just the two of you?" Mustang shook his head. "Where's Gus?"

"He stayed behind with the PI and called for the police and an ambulance."

"Is Phillips still alive?" Mustang asked.

"He had a pulse, but he's pretty banged up and he wasn't wearing a helmet. I don't know if he'll make it."

Mustang took in a deep breath and slowly released it. "I didn't lay eyes on all of the men who followed us into the warehouse, but I would guess there were three or four by the sound of their footsteps. You'll be outnumbered."

"Only three?" Declan's teeth flashed in a grin in the shadowed hall. "Remember that time we were outnumbered twenty to six?"

"We're not in Afghanistan," Mustang reminded him.

"Yeah," Declan said. "But I heard gunfire earlier. I'll be dammed if I let those bastards take potshots at my men. Stay with Emily. We've got this." Declan took off running toward the other end of the hallway.

Mack and Snow followed. They disappeared through what appeared to be another stairwell.

Mustang entered the office and locked the door behind him. He'd have to wait until Declan returned before he could leave with Emily.

"Did I hear right?" her voice sounded in the darkness.

"Hear what?"

"Jay Phillips might not pull through?" she said, her voice catching.

"You saw what happened," Mustang reminded her. "He flew through the air. And he wasn't wearing a helmet. The landing itself could have killed him, even if the impact of the car hitting him didn't." He realized how harsh he sounded and added, "Gus is with him. He called an ambulance and the police. He will stay with Phillips to protect him until they arrive."

He crossed the room to stand in front of her shadowy figure, wishing he could see her face and the expression in her eyes.

"It's just… He didn't do anything to warrant being killed," Emily said, her voice so soft and ragged Mustang barely understood her words. "It's not fair."

"And all you did was interpret for him and witness a man being led around the embassy. A man who is now conveniently missing. You don't deserve to die any more than Phillips or Blunt," Mustang reminded her. He pulled her into his arms.

Emily melted against him, her cheek on his chest, her arms going around his waist. "How many people will be hurt by these people?" Her fingers curled into Mustang's shirt.

"I don't know," he said and smoothed his hand over her soft hair.

"When is this going to end?" she whispered.

"Soon, sweetheart," he assured her, though he had no idea when that might be. He held her for a long time, wishing he could hold her forever and protect her from all the troubles that might come her way. He'd only known her for such a short time, but his attraction to her was so strong he couldn't deny it.

"Mustang?" A soft tap on the door sounded, pulling Mustang back to reality. He stepped away from Emily and went to the door.

Declan, Snow and Mack stood in the hallway. Declan had a flashlight, the beam casting a bright glow in the dark interior of the abandoned warehouse's corridor.

"We didn't see any sign of your attackers anywhere. We checked throughout the warehouse and every one of the offices attached. We even performed a perimeter check of the exterior. The police have arrived."

Emily stepped up beside Mustang.

He slipped his arm around her waist and she leaned into him.

"Has the ambulance arrived?" she asked.

Mack nodded. "It has. They loaded Phillips into it and had him hooked up to oxygen and an IV as they left for the hospital. Gus rode with him in the back of the ambulance."

"Come on," Declan said. "Let's get you back to the Halverson estate before anything else happens."

Mustang couldn't agree with his team leader more.

"I'd rather go to the hospital and check on Jay's status," Emily said.

"Gus will be there with him. He'll keep us informed of Phillips's progress," Declan assured her. "You'll be better off at the estate. You don't want to put anyone else in danger of becoming collateral damage if the attackers follow you to the hospital."

"They could go after Jay," Emily pointed out.

"He's out of it for now. He won't be talking to anyone anytime soon."

"Did anyone collect the backpack he was wearing?" Mustang asked. "He had a tablet inside it with a photo that could help us understand what's going on. He sent it to us, but the tablet might have more."

Mack turned around and jerked his thumb over his shoulder. "You mean this backpack?"

Mustang nodded. "Have you checked the contents? Was the tablet still inside?"

Mack slipped the straps off his shoulders and opened the backpack, from which he pulled the device, its screen shattered. "Let's get it back to Cole and Charlie's computer guy. They should be able to hack into the device and retrieve the data."

They spent an hour with the police, giving a detailed description of what had taken place, describing the van that had hit Jay Phillips and then rammed the car Mustang had been driving into the warehouse.

Mustang made certain Emily was allowed to sit in the back seat of Declan's vehicle throughout the questioning. He wasn't going to leave her exposed anymore than he had to. When the police were done with them, he climbed in next to her and pulled her against his side.

Declan and Mack rode up front, each watching for trouble at intersections and keeping an eye on the rearview mirror.

By the time they passed through the gate at the Halverson estate, Emily had fallen asleep against Mustang's chest.

Declan pulled up to the front of the house and parked just as Arnold appeared, opened the door to the truck and helped Emily down. Still groggy, she stumbled on the first step.

Mustang swept her into his arms and carried her into the house and up the steps to the bedroom he would share with her that night.

"I can walk, you know," she said, though she snuggled into him rather than struggled to be free.

"I know, but it's faster this way. Besides, you have to be exhausted."

"No more so than you."

He shook his head. "I can go several days without sleep and still function."

She yawned into his shirt. "I don't know how you do it."

He deposited her on her feet in the bedroom, closed and locked the door and then pushed the chair against the French doors and another in front of her hallway door, as he had the night before. Just the thought of her standing out on the balcony and being pushed over the edge made his skin crawl. He shuddered at the mental image. He checked under the bed, in the closet and in the bathroom before declaring, "The room is safe."

"Good." Emily smiled. "I'm not sure I have the energy to fight off an intruder at this point. I'm going to get another shower. After running through that abandoned warehouse, I feel like I picked up several pounds of dust." She gathered clothes and ducked into the bathroom.

Mustang entered the adjoining room, leaving the door open between them. He jumped in his shower and rinsed off, straining the entire time to hear even the slightest sound from the other room. Once he finished, he toweled dry and slipped into a pair of shorts he'd sleep in. Normally he slept naked, but he figured sleeping in the nude was pushing the boundaries of the new relationship between himself and Emily. Yes, they shared an amazing kiss, but expecting it to progress to sleeping together naked was presuming too much.

He pulled a T-shirt over his head as he entered Emily's bedroom.

The shower was still going, but soon shut off. A few minutes later the door opened and Emily stepped out, wearing a fluffy, white, terry-cloth robe, her long legs bare below the hem.

Mustang's groin tightened.

She'd combed her damp hair straight back from her forehead and her cheeks were clean and pink from the hot shower. As she stood in front of him, her cheeks grew even pinker. Emily tugged at the terry-cloth belt around her waist and cleared her throat. "I'm tired, but I doubt I'll sleep much." She shifted her gaze from his and looked around the room. "Why don't you take the bed and I'll sleep in the chair?"

He shook his head. "It's your bed. You need the sleep more than I do."

Her lips twisted. "But you didn't sleep much last night. Even marines have to recharge their bodies."

"I catnap. It's enough."

"Bull feathers," she exclaimed. "If you won't take the bed by yourself, then at least sleep in it with me." She lifted her chin. "I'll stay on my side. You won't even know I'm there."

Mustang snorted. "Sweetheart, I'll know you're there. Hell, I'd know you were anywhere in the same room." He shook his head again. "I can't sleep with you."

She frowned. "Why?"

He captured her gaze with a hard one of his own. "Because if I sleep in the same bed as you, I won't be able to keep my hands to myself. It's best if I sleep in the chair."

Her eyes widened and her tongue swept across her lips as if they'd suddenly gone dry. For a long moment she just stared into his eyes. Then she whispered, "What if I don't want you to keep your hands to yourself?"

Mustang closed his eyes tightly to block the image of her standing there in that robe, the valley of her breasts visible in the neckline and her long legs so tantalizingly toned and silky. "I don't think it's a good idea."

Gentle hands touched his chest.

He blinked open his eyes and stared down into Emily's eyes.

"Funny, but I think it's the best idea we've had all day." Her words came out warm and husky, melting into every pore of Mustang's body.

He gripped her arms.

That was his first mistake.

Pulling her close was his downfall.

The terry cloth did little to disguise the curves of her body beneath the robe as she pressed against him.

A groan rose in his throat. "Emily, I'm supposed to protect you, not take advantage of you." He knew he should push her away and take a step back, but his hands refused his brain's logic.

"I think *I'm* the one taking advantage of *you*." She lifted up on her toes and pressed her lips to his in a gentle kiss.

When her mouth touched his, a firestorm of sensations blasted through his veins. He slid his hands down her arms and onto her hips, pulling her even closer. "I'm barely fit to be around people after being at war for so long," he said, burying his face in her hair.

She chuckled, the sound like silk sliding across his skin. "I've been so busy building my career, I don't even know how to be with a man. You might find me...lacking in experience."

He leaned back and smoothed a strand of her hair out of her face. "Sweetheart, you're pushing all my buttons, so you must be doing something right." Then he kissed her, taking her mouth in a long, sensuous caress.

When she opened to him and returned the kiss, they were closer than they'd ever been and yet he felt as if he couldn't get close enough.

When he finally came up for air, Emily slipped her hands between them and untied the belt on her robe. She stepped back and let the garment fall open, revealing that she wore nothing beneath.

Another groan slipped along Mustang's throat. He cupped her chin and tilted her head up to his. "Are you sure this is what you want?"

She nodded. "I left my nightgown in the bathroom...on purpose." She tilted her head and raised her eyebrows in a challenge he couldn't refuse.

"If at any time you feel uncomfortable, just say the word and I'll back off," he said, already pushing the robe from her shoulders. He paused with his hands on the terry cloth, a frown pulling his brow low. "Wait."

Emily's brow knit in confusion. "For what? I thought it was settled."

He grinned and left her standing in her room to race into his. It took him thirty precious seconds to locate what he needed and return to where they'd left off.

Emily had pulled her robe back up over her shoulders and closed the edges. "Did *you* change your mind? I don't want you to feel any obligation toward me other than protecting me. I hope I didn't push you into a corner. Like you said…if you feel at all uncomfortable, I'll back off."

Mustang laughed and pressed a finger to her lips. "Shh. I haven't changed my mind, but we couldn't go any further without this." He lifted her hand and dropped an accordion of condoms into her palm. "I don't want you to have any regrets."

"My only regret is that we didn't get started sooner." She tossed the condoms on the bed and wrapped her arms around his neck. "Hold me, Mustang. I need to feel your body against mine."

Her words echoed Mustang's own thoughts. He pulled her against him and scooped her up by the backs of her thighs, wrapping those long, sexy legs around his waist. The robe swung around them.

Emily removed her arms from around Mustang's neck and shrugged out of the robe over her shoulders. "I'm not experienced in the art of seduction," she said, "but I learn quickly." The robe dropped to the floor.

He walked her to the bed and set her down on the edge, running his hands from her hips into the curves of her waist and up to cup the swells of her breasts in his palms.

She tightened her legs around his middle and arched her back, pressing against his hands.

Mustang pulled back long enough to yank his shirt over his head.

Emily dropped her legs over the side of the bed and sat up. She pressed her lips to his naked ribs, kissing him there and flicking her tongue against his skin. All the while her hands got busy in the elastic of his shorts. She slipped inside them to cup his backside, pulling him closer. Then she worked his shorts over his hips and down his thighs, easing his erection free in the process.

Impatience won out and Mustang shimmied free of his shorts and stepped out of them to stand naked in front of Emily.

She smiled, her lips forming a seductive curl.

He laid her back and parted her thighs, kissing a path from the bend of her knee to her center.

In less than two days he'd come to care for this woman. Not because she was the job, but because she was smart, sexy and courageous in the face of a deadly threat. She didn't care that he wasn't in the military anymore. It wasn't even a factor as she hadn't known him when he'd been a marine. She wanted him for who he was now.

Mustang parted her folds and thumbed the

nubbin he knew would bring her pleasure, really wanting her to like making love to him. He wanted that so much because he couldn't see one time being nearly enough.

WHEN MUSTANG TOUCHED his tongue to that special place, Emily let out a small cry of passion and dug her heels into the mattress, lifting her bottom up. "Please," she said.

"Please what?" Mustang asked, blowing a warm stream of air across that fevered strip of flesh.

"Please, I want more," she moaned, letting her knees drop to the sides, opening herself to him.

He tongued her again, setting off an explosion of nerves that originated at her core and spread outward to the very tips of her extremities.

Emily weaved her hands into his hair and held on until the wave crested and ebbed. Then she pulled on his hair, urging him to give more.

Mustang climbed up the bed and settled between her legs, the tip of his shaft pressing against her entrance. There, he paused and searched the bed for the strip of condoms. When he found it, he leaned up on his knees, tore off one and ripped it open.

Emily took the condom from his hands and

rolled it down over his erection, stopped at the base to fondle him. She loved how hard his shaft was in her hand and shivered at the thought of him inside her. And then it couldn't happen soon enough. She tugged on him, guiding him to her. When he touched her there, she shifted her hands to his hips and pulled him into her.

He fit tightly, his girth stretching her deliciously.

Once he'd entered her with his full length, he pulled almost all the way out and drove in again, settling into a smooth, sensuous rhythm.

Emily pressed her feet into the comforter and lifted up, meeting every one of Mustang's thrusts, driving him even deeper.

His body tensed. He dragged in a deep, ragged breath, thrust one last time and held himself there, filling her so completely, she tipped over the edge again and came undone.

His shaft throbbed inside her as her body shook with the force of her release.

When at last she fell back to earth, she lay limp against the mattress, drained and completely satisfied. For the moment.

Mustang dropped down and rolled both of them onto their sides, maintaining their intimate connection.

A chuckle escaped Emily's throat.

Mustang leaned up on his elbow and frowned down at her. "I was expecting a wow, not laughter. Was it that bad?"

She cupped his cheek in her hand. "Not at all. Quite the opposite. I was just realizing how much I've missed all those years of studying and furthering my career. And, wow." Emily shook her head. "Just wow. I really didn't know it could be so good."

Mustang brushed a kiss across her forehead. "Can't tell you how relieved I am to hear that. You had me worried."

"Trust me, sweetheart," Emily said, "you have nothing to worry about. If you treat all your women that way, you'll have no troubles finding one to warm your bed." Her heart squeezed as she spoke the words. Mustang hadn't said he was committing the rest of his life to be with her. Hell, they barely knew each other. At the least, she might have him for a couple more days. After they resolved her attacker issue, Mustang was under no obligation to continue their connection.

The thought of leaving Mustang behind made Emily's chest tighten and a lead weight settle in her gut. He'd become such a part of her life in the past two days, she couldn't imagine a future without him.

But what would keep them together?

Chapter Fifteen

Mustang lay long into the night without falling asleep. His time with Emily had taken an altogether different path than he'd ever imagined. A path he didn't want to see come to an end. Especially such a permanent end as death.

If her attacker managed to slip by him and his team, she could be dead within a week. Heck, within the next twenty-four hours.

His fists clenched. Losing her was not an option. He'd risk his own life to save her. The woman had so much to offer the world in intelligence and kindness.

By the time the sun crept through the gaps in the blinds, Mustang was up and pacing the length of the room, trying to figure out how to capture the attacker without putting Emily up as bait.

"Hey," a soft voice called out.

Mustang stopped halfway across the room and turned to the woman lying in the bed, her hair rumpled and her cheeks flushed with sleep. God, she was beautiful.

He wanted to go to her and make love to her all over again, but the worry eating at his gut kept him at a distance. He knew if he touched her, he wouldn't be able to resist. And he needed a clear mind and a hell of a lot of focus to see this job through. And when it was over… when the attacker was captured and Emily was safe again, then Mustang would start over and woo this beautiful professor the proper way.

She reached out a slender arm and the comforter slipped lower, exposing a tempting breast.

Mustang swallowed a moan and turned away. "I'll leave you to get dressed. We need to come up with a plan today."

"Is it something I said?" she asked.

He turned back to her. "No, it's something we have to do before this can go any further."

She sat up, pulling the comforter over her chest, her cheeks turning a pretty shade of pink. "Having second thoughts?" She trapped her bottom lip between her teeth, a frown furrowing her brow.

"Far from it. Until we find out who is attacking you, I need to keep my focus."

Her frown smoothed and a smile curled the

corners of her lips. "And I make you lose focus?" She chuckled. "I suppose that's a compliment."

"Damn right, it's a compliment." He stood in the middle of the room, staring at her, wishing the circumstances were different. "Please," he said. "Just get dressed. I'll be in the other room." He marched out of her bedroom, refusing to look back.

Her soft laughter followed him.

He could hear her moving around, opening the bathroom door, the sound of water running and the tap of a toothbrush against the porcelain sink.

He was so aware of her, he could imagine everything she was doing.

Finally she appeared in the door frame of the adjoining room, buttoning the front of a soft pink blouse she wore with a pair of gray trousers. "Just so you know," she said, "you make me lose focus, too. But I don't necessarily consider it a bad thing."

"It would be bad in my case if my loss of focus left you vulnerable to attack." He nodded at her bare feet. "I'd wear something comfortable."

One side of her mouth lifted in a sardonic grin. "In case I have to run?"

He nodded. "Precisely."

She disappeared into her room and came

back wearing a pair of black-leather flats and carrying her cell phone. "Will these do?"

He nodded. "Let's get downstairs and see if Cole's made any progress on locating the hotel where Phillips snapped that photo." He strode to the bedroom door, pulled the chair away and yanked it open. He stood back as Emily passed so close he could smell the scent of her shampoo.

She leaned closer. "Your focus is slipping." Emily's grin spread across her face as she walked ahead of him to the top of the staircase.

He hurried past her to take the lead, descending to the main level.

He followed the voices emanating from the dining room.

Declan gave him a chin lift as he entered. "Oh, good, we were just about to come get you."

"What have you found?" Mustang held a chair for Emily and waited for her to be seated before claiming the chair beside her.

Charlie, Grace, Jonah and Cole sat at the table with half-eaten plates of food in front of them.

"Jonah and Cole were able to hack into Phillips's tablet and retrieve the digital images. We found the one you were talking about that showed Blunt and the ambassador's daughter with Viktor Sokolov in the alley in the background."

Mustang paused in the middle of scooping scrambled eggs onto his plate. "And?"

"We think we know where they were," Cole said.

"The Trinity Hotel." Jonah jabbed his fork at a piece of chicken. "It's located in Alexandria."

Emily pushed back her chair. "Well, let's go check it out."

Mustang grabbed her arm and urged her to take her seat. "Not without a plan. And I'm not so sure you need to go. Declan and the others can check it out. You and I can stay put until they return with whatever they find out."

Emily scowled. "I'm not good at sitting around doing nothing."

"Then you can work with Jonah as he hacks into the embassy database," Charlie said.

Jonah nodded. "I understand you understand Russian. All the information in that database might as well be Greek to me."

Emily seemed to consider the prospect. "You'll let us know what you find, as soon as you find anything?"

Declan held up his hand as if swearing before a judge. "Promise."

"Okay." Emily settled back in her seat. "I'll

stay and translate." But she didn't look all that happy about being left behind.

Mustang was more than relieved. He could keep a closer watch on her if she stayed inside the house. But he knew he wouldn't be able to keep her housebound for long. The woman had a life and she'd refuse to be held captive for any length of time.

Grace reached over and covered Emily's hand. "The guys are only trying to keep you safe."

Emily sighed. "I know. I'm not used to being the target of some nut job. If I knew who it was, I'd confront him."

"No, we'd send the police after him," Charlie said. "Whoever these people are, they are playing for keeps. You're not trained in warfare. That's why we have Declan's Defenders. They'll help keep you safe, if you let them."

Mustang wanted to cheer Charlie for her comments, but he kept quiet, letting her words sink in with Emily.

"You're right," she said. "And I'm grateful for all you've done for me. I wouldn't be alive today without their help." She slipped her hand beneath the table and captured Mustang's, giving it a squeeze.

After a quick breakfast, Declan and Cole

left the estate, destined for the Trinity Hotel in Alexandria.

Emily and Mustang helped carry dishes into the kitchen where the chef and his staff made quick work of cleaning up.

Jonah led them to the computer room where he had an array of six monitors lined up in front of a single keyboard. He tapped on the keys and brought up a screen filled with files all labeled in Russian.

For the next two hours Emily translated file names and searched through data on the Russian embassy's database. For all the work, they came up with nothing substantial. Names of people, biographies of individuals, schedules of visiting diplomats and records of Russian ships entering American ports all over the US, including some in the DC, Maryland and Virginia area. Nothing jumped out at them as being something that could help them determine who was after her and Jay Phillips or why.

Emily pinched the bridge of her nose and stood. "I need something for a headache."

"Let's take a break." Mustang walked with her to the kitchen where the chef offered them a cup of coffee or hot tea.

"I'd like the tea," Emily said.

"I could use some coffee."

They collected their steaming cups and sat at the solid-oak kitchen table. No sooner had they taken their seats than Emily's cell phone buzzed with an incoming text message.

She glanced down, a frown forming on her brow. "It's from Sachi Kozlov."

Mustang leaned over her shoulder and read the message.

Found Tyler's journal. You need to see this. Meet me at DC's Eastern Flea Market at 2:00 pm. I'll be at the Crepes food truck wearing a gold scarf.

Emily checked the time on her cell phone. "That gives us an hour to get there and find her."

"Us?" Mustang shook his head. "I don't feel good about you being out and about. What if this is a setup? We just did a meeting that didn't end well. Call her back. Ask what's up."

"I'm not calling her back. If she wants to meet, it could be because talking on the phone is difficult. People might be nearby she doesn't want eavesdropping. I won't do anything that might put her at risk."

"I don't like doing anything that puts you at risk," he countered.

"I can go in a disguise," Emily said. "I'm

going. You can come with me or not." She responded to Sachi's text.

I will be there.

Mustang already knew he wasn't going to talk Emily out of going. "Fine. But we will have to make your disguise good enough to fool the best. Where's Grace?" He stood and held her chair for her.

She rose and hurried through the house. "Grace? Charlie? I need your help."

Meanwhile, Mustang was on his cell phone clicking on his team lead's number. "Declan, I need your help."

AT PRECISELY 1:58 P.M. EMILY, dressed in baggy jeans and a hooded sweatshirt with the hood pulled up over her hair, stood twenty yards from the Crepes food truck at DC's Flea Market at Eastern Market, searching for a woman in a gold scarf. "I don't see her," she said to Mustang, who stood beside her, wearing a similar outfit, his hands in his jacket pocket, resting on his handgun.

"It's not quite two. Give her a minute," he said softly.

From around the other side of the rendezvous truck, a woman emerged, dressed in a gray trench coat and a gold scarf.

Emily's heart beat fast. "There she is." She stepped forward but Mustang's hand held her back.

"Wait a moment in case she was followed." He scanned the area, searching for anyone watching Sachi and her movements.

Emily kept her head down to disguise the fact she wasn't the teenaged boy she was dressed as. She'd scrubbed her face, pulled back her hair and tucked it into the hoodie she'd brought for her disguise. She'd had Grace and Charlie give her thicker eyebrows. Charlie had invested in costume makeup on the off chance Declan's Defenders needed to disguise themselves. She'd been excited that they would actually put the makeup to use for a good cause… keeping Emily safe. Charlie had also found the hooded sweatshirt and helped Emily into it. Then Charlie had hugged her. "Don't lose the hoodie. It will help us find you."

They'd left the estate in the back of a delivery van and caught a taxi once they'd arrived in the DC city limits. They had the taxi drop them off several blocks from the flea market and walked the rest of the way like two guys just hanging out.

"Well?" Emily asked. "Is it safe?"

"I can only hope so. I don't see any suspicious characters."

Sachi had settled into a seat at one of the bistro tables with her back to a shade tree, her face and body cloaked in the shadows.

"We'll order a crepe before we engage with Sachi. Stay close to me," Mustang ordered.

"No argument here," Emily said in her gruffest guy-voice.

They walked over to the crepe truck. Mustang ordered a crepe with strawberries.

Emily stood beside him, watching Sachi out of the corner of her eye.

The woman pulled her scarf over the lower half of her face, but her ice-blue eyes were unforgettable and gave her away.

"I'm going to join her," Emily said.

"Wait for me. It will look more natural if we both sit together. The other tables are filling up."

Emily saw reason and waited for the man in the food truck to finish making the strawberry crepe. Then she and Mustang looked around as if searching for an empty table and not finding it. Sachi's table was the only one with a single occupant.

Mustang carried his plate with the strawberry crepe and stopped in front of Sachi. "Mind if we share your table?"

The Russian ambassador's daughter started to shake her head. "I'm sorry, but I'm waiting for someone."

Emily looked down at Sachi, willing her to recognize her despite the disguise. Finally she whispered. "It's me, Emily."

Sachi's gaze darted to Emily's eyes. Her own narrowed. Then she glanced around nervously and nodded, her gaze lighting on Mustang, whom she seemed to remember from the classroom visit. She relaxed a little. "Please, take a seat." She shifted her chair to make room for them.

"I'll eat, you two talk." Mustang cut off a piece of the crepe and popped it into his mouth.

Sachi glanced down at the purse in her lap. "This was one of the places Tyler and I would meet when I could escape my bodyguards. It's easy to blend into the crowd, as long as I change the color of my scarf. The trick was to wear something unmemorable besides the scarf." Her hand fluttered to the gold cloth. "But that is not the reason I asked you to come." She shifted in her seat and unzipped her oversize purse. "I found these in the safe deposit box Tyler and I share at a local bank. They're the journals he kept when he was doing an investigation."

"Did you find anything about you or the

Russian embassy in it?" Emily asked softly, barely moving her lips lest someone see her talking to the stranger.

Sachi nodded, almost imperceptibly. "He was following a story about human trafficking in the DC area. He wrote that he suspected someone in the Russian embassy was responsible for transporting women out of the US." She pulled a small leather-bound journal out of her voluminous bag and pushed it across the table. "I bent the page where Tyler noted that he suspected one of the higher-ranking embassy staff was involved. He'd seen the man outside a hotel with a very young woman who'd appeared to stagger and drag her feet, maybe drugged.

"He'd gone back to that hotel and asked questions of the staff, most of whom knew nothing about any potential human trafficking going on beneath their roof. But some of them were less talkative and more guarded. Tyler had planned a stakeout to capture more evidence on video. He'd even given up a chance to be with me in order to gather the evidence he needed to turn the mastermind behind the human trafficking in to the authorities.

"That had been the night before. Since then, Tyler has disappeared." Sachi's voice faded into a silent sob. "I don't know where he is or who took him."

"Sachi, I was at the embassy two days ago, interpreting for your father. I saw Tyler Blunt there."

The other woman's eyes grew wide. "You saw him? That was the day he disappeared."

"Your father was very angry about your relationship with the journalist," Emily said. "He stormed out of the meeting, shouting."

Sachi shook her head. "He came to me and told me that I had to break up with Tyler. I told him that I would not. I would leave the embassy and him if he banned me from seeing the man I love."

"What did he say?"

"He threatened to pay Tyler to quit seeing me. I told my father I would never speak to him again if he damaged my relationship with Tyler."

"Is your father capable of kidnapping and potentially murdering?" Emily asked quietly.

Sachi shook her head. "I've known my father to get very angry, but he has never hurt another human being. I don't think he would hurt Tyler."

"Have you ever suspected your father of having any dealings with the buying and selling of women to other countries for profit?" Mustang asked between bites of the crepe.

Sachi's eyes opened even wider. "No. Of

course not. He was very much in love with my mother, and he's been a good father, so very protective of the women in his family and on his staff. He would never hurt another woman. His anger is legendary, but his kindness is equally revered." She glanced down at her watch. "I've told you all I know. Now I have to get back to my bodyguards before they call my father or send out a search party."

Emily wanted to ask more questions but the woman was clearly packing up her things to leave. "Let us escort you back to your people," Emily offered.

Sachi frowned. "I don't know. It might be better if I show up alone."

"Please," Emily implored. "With so many attempts on my life, what if the information you just passed on to us is what our attackers are after? That could place you in just as much danger as myself and the private investigator who was assigned to follow you and Tyler around."

"No one knows that I know about Tyler's journal and its contents besides you two."

"I'd feel better if we followed you back. You know the investigator is in the hospital?"

"The private investigator who was following us?" Sachi asked. "No, I did not."

"Someone broadsided him on his motorcycle last night and then tried to hit us, as well."

Sachi's hand fluttered over the scarf. "I did not know. Will he live?"

Emily shook her head. "Only time will tell. He was still unconscious, the last word I received."

Sachi shook her head. "I hope he recovers. And, yes, I would like you to follow me, but not so close that it appears obvious to onlookers."

Mustang tossed his crepe into a trash bin as he followed Emily and Sachi from the food truck.

Emily hurried after Sachi, afraid she'd get too far ahead of them to provide any kind of protection should someone try to harm her.

The ambassador's daughter wove her way through the throngs of people milling about the flea market, until she emerged along another street where a homeless man dug in a trash can and a black limousine stood ten yards farther against the curb.

Sachi didn't slow until she reached the limousine.

Emily watched as Sachi came to a stop in front of one of the bodyguards. She frowned heavily at the big, burly man standing at the rear door of the limousine. Then she backed away quickly.

The man caught her arm and yanked her against him. And just like that, the situation went to hell.

Sachi screamed and struggled against the big guy's grip on her.

Emily leaped forward, racing toward Sachi, too far away to be of any real assistance. But she couldn't stand by and do nothing.

Sachi was forced into the back of the limousine.

"Emily," Mustang called out, his footsteps pounding on the ground behind her.

She couldn't stop. Sachi was in trouble and they'd promised to see her safely to her people. The man at the limousine had obviously not been one of her regular bodyguards.

As Emily and Mustang reached the limousine, the burly guy had already slammed the door and was moving toward the front passenger door.

"Hey!" Emily called out.

The man turned and faced her.

Mustang caught up with her before she reached the big man who'd shoved Sachi into the limousine.

Still more footsteps sounded behind Emily and Mustang.

Mustang spun, but not soon enough to block the steel pipe that crashed down at the base of his skull. He went down and lay as still as death at Emily's feet.

"Mustang?" she cried and dove for the man who'd saved her life on more than one occasion.

A hand caught her hair before she hit the ground and yanked her back.

She screamed and fought, but the man holding her hair clamped strong arms around her middle and lifted her off the ground.

The man who'd wrestled with Sachi pulled open the door to the back seat. Emily was deposited like a sack of potatoes onto the floorboard and the door was slammed shut behind her.

Sachi lay on the floor, sobbing.

"Are these your bodyguards?" Emily demanded.

Sachi shook her head. "I've never seen these men before."

Emily found the door handle and pulled hard, but the door wouldn't open. The locks were obviously controlled by the driver up front. She pounded her fists against the glass windows but they didn't break.

And Mustang lay on the ground, unmoving. Was he dead?

Oh, dear God, Emily prayed. *Please let him live.*

The limousine pulled away, rounded a corner and left Mustang behind.

Chapter Sixteen

"Hey, mister," a voice said through the fog of Mustang's brain.

Mustang blinked his eyes open and stared sideways at what appeared to be dirt and shoes.

A man squatted beside him and peered into his eyes. "Are you okay? Should I call an ambulance?"

"What happened?"

The man shook his head. "I don't know. I just found you lying here, unconscious. You have a heck of a goose egg on the back of your head and it's bleeding a little. I'm going to call an ambulance." He pulled out his cell phone and looked down at the screen.

"No," Mustang said and pushed to his hands and knees. Pain ripped through the back of his skull and reverberated throughout his head. His thoughts were just starting to gel when he remembered. "Emily." He staggered to his feet and swayed. "Two women. Did you see them?"

The man shook his head, a frown denting his forehead. "No. Just you." He looked around. "No women. I really think you need to see a doctor. You could have a concussion."

Mustang started to shake his head and thought better of it. "No, thank you. I'll be okay. I have to go." He fished in his pocket for his cell phone and punched Declan's number.

Declan answered immediately. "Mustang, where are you? We just arrived at the flea market."

"They're gone," he said, his stomach roiling, his head throbbing with pain and regret.

"What do you mean they're gone?" Declan asked.

"We were escorting Sachi back to her vehicle when someone hit me from behind." He pressed a hand to the back of his head and winced when it came into contact with the goose-egg-size lump at the base of his skull. "I don't know how long I've been out, but they're gone. Nowhere to be seen."

"I'm at the entrance to the market by the kettle corn booth. Do you need me to call an ambulance?"

"I don't need an ambulance," Mustang bit

out. "I need to find Emily." He sprinted toward the entrance. "I'm on my way to you."

Minutes later he met up with Declan and Cole.

"I let Charlie know what was happening," Declan said. "We're in luck. The hooded sweatshirt she gave Emily to wear had a GPS tracking chip in the pocket." Declan shook his head. "That woman knows all the tricks. Cole will forward the link to her tracker. Mack, Gus and Snow are on their way. They're bringing firepower, as well."

A huge wave of relief washed over Mustang for all of a split second. Sure, they might find her, but would it be too late?

A few moments later he climbed into Declan's truck and settled back against the passenger seat. Cole got into the back seat.

How had he let this happen? Mustang had seen the limousine and the man who'd shoved Sachi inside. Otherwise, the street had been fairly empty. Where had the man come from who'd hit him in the back of the head? An image flashed in his mind, one of a homeless man digging in the trash near the limousine. Had he been a decoy? Did it matter? The fact was, Emily and Sachi had been taken. He'd bet the men with the limousine weren't her regular bodyguards. She hadn't gone into the vehicle willingly. Mustang was sure Emily wouldn't have gotten in without a fight.

A text came in on Declan's cell phone. He handed it to Mustang. "I'll drive. You communicate."

Mustang read the text out loud. "'Heading to Baltimore on Interstate Highway 295. About one hour ahead of us.'" He frowned. "Why would they go to Baltimore?"

"Guess we're going to find out," Declan said, pressing his foot down hard on the accelerator as he merged onto Highway 295 heading out of DC. Traffic was thick, but not as bad as on a regular workday.

Declan broke all the speed limits, weaving in between cars and eighteen wheelers. They made record time up the highway and probably cut the usual travel time nearly by half.

As they approached Baltimore, another text came through.

Mustang read it. "'Take Interstate 895 to the 695 south bypass.'"

Declan followed the directions. "Mack and the others must be a good fifteen minutes ahead of us."

Mustang nodded, his mind on the road ahead and every potential scenario he could imagine.

"She'll be okay," Declan assured him.

Cole leaned over the back seat and tapped Mustang's shoulder. "We'll get her out of this."

Mustang couldn't respond. He'd let her down. Failed in his duty to protect her. But he couldn't dwell on that. Getting her back alive was his goal. Failure on this mission wasn't an option.

Declan's cell phone rang with Mack's Caller ID on the display screen.

Declan answered via the Bluetooth option on his truck.

Mack's voice sounded over the speaker. "The tracker has slowed considerably and, get this…they're in the Baltimore shipyard. We're not close enough yet to see what terrain we'll have to deal with, but we'll get as close as we can and wait for you to catch up."

"Roger," Declan said. "We should be there in approximately fifteen minutes."

"Where the hell are they taking them?" Mustang muttered.

Declan shook his head and increased their speed. "I don't know, but it can't be good."

THE LIMOUSINE'S WINDOWS had been blackened, not allowing the passengers a view of where they were going. When the vehicle finally stopped, Emily and Sachi were ready to fight for their escape. As soon as the door opened,

Emily dove out onto concrete and rolled across the ground. She was up on her feet and ready to run, but she was captured before she could take two steps. Someone with beefy arms caught her around the middle. Dusk had settled in early with an overcast sky, making it difficult to ascertain where she was. All she could see were tall stacks of metal freight containers.

She screamed as loud as she could. It bought her a dirty rag in her mouth and a sack over her head. Then she was flung over her captor's shoulder, her legs clamped tightly by his arm. No matter how much she tried to kick and buck, she couldn't free herself from her stronger captor. She was carried across a long, flat area. Then her abductor was walking across something that wasn't concrete. His footsteps clanged on what sounded like metal, maybe a bridge, and then he stepped down onto another surface.

Emily strained to make out this new sound. Again, it could have been metal, only it wasn't as hollow as the clanging noise. Where had they taken her and Sachi? Muffled sobbing reassured her that Sachi was still with her, even if they were both still kept captive.

She was carried down metal steps and still more steps. Finally the clang of metal against metal indicated a door being opened. With all the sounds of metal, and the shipping containers she'd seen when she'd attempted her escape, Emily had to conclude they had been taken on board a ship. She could smell and hear the lapping of waves.

Her heart constricted and her pulse raced. Escaping from solid walls and doors of a ship would be much more difficult than if she'd been taken to a building. And if the ship went out to sea, there was the matter of where she could escape to.

Emily was dumped on the floor. Someone else landed beside her with an *umph*.

By the time she pulled the sack off her head and the rag from her mouth, the door to her new cell closed and the sound of gears turning on the other side indicated it had been sealed.

Darkness surrounded her. There was no portal and no light leaked around the edges of the door as it was doubtlessly designed to be watertight. That was probably why they'd not bound their hands. Why bother when they were dumping them in this light-deprived cell?

"Sachi?" Emily whispered.

"*Da*," Sachi responded, her voice catching on a sob. "Where are we?"

"I think we're on board a ship." Emily sat on a hard metal floor. This wasn't a cruise ship with carpeting and soft, comfy beds. Since it was located near a shipyard with containers, it was probably a no-frills freighter. She felt her way around the room. Their cell was completely empty, nothing but a box in which to contain them.

"We have to get out of here," Emily said, fighting the feeling that the walls were closing in around her.

"How?" Sachi sniffed.

"There has to be a handle on the door. We just have to find it."

Emily ran her hands along the walls until she located the edges of the door. She found a wheel handle in the middle and tried to turn it. No matter how hard she pulled on it in either direction, it would not budge. "It must be locked from the other side."

She sat next to Sachi, took her hand in hers and tried to think of a way to break the lock. With nothing harder than the clothes they were wearing or the sacks they'd had pulled over their heads, they had no way to break through the door or to apply leverage to the wheel handle. The only way out was if someone let them out.

Emily sighed. "We'll have to wait until someone opens the door. But we should be ready."

"Tell me how," Sachi said. "I'll help."

Emily handed her one of the bags their captors had used to subdue them with. "Rip this into long strips."

"What are we going to do with them?" Sachi asked.

"I have a plan but we need to act fast." She took the other bag and tore lengths of two-inch-wide strips. Once they had both bags torn up, she tied the strips together into two long ropes.

"We'll position ourselves on either side of the door, but out of sight as much as possible. When someone comes through the door to look for us, we'll use one rope to trip him and the other to tie him up."

"What if there is more than one?" Sachi asked.

"Then we trip the second one through the door. He'll fall into the first one and we'll make our escape while they're picking themselves up off the floor." The plan was weak at best, and it would only work if someone came through their door.

For the next thirty minutes they sat on either side of the door, waiting in the dark.

"My father thinks my relationship with Tyler is just a passing fling," Sachi whispered.

"And how do you feel?" Emily asked softly.

"If he asks me to marry him, I will. I love him with all my heart."

Emily thought of how long she'd known Mustang and how much he was already a part of her life. She didn't want to think about their eventual parting. She'd never felt that way about any man. And she'd only been with him for two short days. "How long have you known each other?"

Sachi laughed. "Two weeks. Two weeks and I know in my heart he's the one for me."

"Does he feel the same?"

She laughed again, the sound catching on a sob. "He told me that he loves me even before I was sure."

"Do you worry that he might be using you to get closer to what's going on at the embassy?"

"No. He said he'd walk away from any story if it would prove to me that he is truly in love with me." She sighed. "I believe him. He's a good man who only wants to report the truth so that bad things can be fixed and the good can be revealed. Just read his articles and listen to his reports. You would know who he is by his work."

"I've seen some of his investigative reports. He's helped a lot of people." Emily hoped for Sachi's sake that Tyler was really in love with her. How did anyone know for sure?

Muffled footsteps sounded in the hallway outside the door to their cell.

"Once the door opens, don't make a sound," Emily whispered. "They have to think we've disappeared."

Emily moved back, away from the door and out of the path of any light that might spill in.

The screech of the wheel handle turning made her pulse leap. This could be their only chance of escape. They had to make it count.

The door swung outward. A yellowish light poured through, illuminating a rectangle across the middle of the small cell. For someone on the outside looking in, the cell might as well be empty.

Emily pressed up against the wall, making herself as small as possible, while holding on to her end of the makeshift rope.

A man spoke in Russian. "This is the room?"

"*Da*," came the answer.

"They are gone."

"*Nyet*. They are in there." A man stepped through the door.

Emily held her breath and prayed Sachi wouldn't get excited and pull the rope too soon.

The second man entered the doorway.

About the time the first man turned and spotted her, Emily yelled, "Now!"

Both women pulled hard on the rope as the second man stepped through.

His foot caught and he pitched forward,

knocking into the man in front of him, hitting him hard enough that both crashed into the opposite wall.

"Go!" Emily cried as she scrambled to her feet.

Sachi dove for the door.

Emily was on her heels.

The ambassador's daughter hesitated in the dim hallway. "Which way?"

Emily slammed the door shut and twisted the wheel handle. Then she shoved a metal locking lever into place before her jailers could recover.

Pounding sounded against the door, making Emily jump back. The men inside shouted, their voices muffled by the thick metal walls.

"Help us!" A feminine cry came from another door farther down the hallway.

"Did you hear that?" Emily asked.

"Someone is crying for help," Sachi said.

Emily ran to the door behind which came the sound of several women crying out for help. She slid the exterior locking lever to the side and spun the wheel handle. Sachi helped her pull the door open. The room was as small as the one they had just escaped. But inside a dozen women were crowded into the cramped space.

A blond-haired, blue-eyed young woman who couldn't have been more than seventeen swayed toward Emily. "Please, help us." Her words were slurred and she seemed barely able to stand.

After a quick glance at the others Emily shook her head. "These women have been drugged."

"Drugs," the blonde said. "They made us take pills."

"We're going to get you out of here," Emily promised.

"Want to go home," the blonde said, tears streaming down her cheeks.

"We'll get you there, but right now you have to think. Are there more of you?"

Three or four of the women closest to Emily nodded.

Emily's heart squeezed hard in her chest. These women were being shipped out of the US, probably to be sold in the sex trade in some foreign country.

Sachi ran to the next door and shoved the locking lever to the side. Emily helped her spin the wheel handle and push open the door. Ten more women sat or lay passed out on the floor.

They went to the next door and opened it. This room appeared empty until a groan sounded from a dark corner.

Emily hurried in.

What appeared to be a pile of dirty clothes

was actually a man. As she neared him, she recognized his pale blue shirt and dark hair. "Tyler? Is that you?"

"Tyler?" Sachi called, muttering a string of curses in Russian as she rushed to his side. "What have they done to you?"

The man lifted his head, exposing a battered face with dried blood from a gash in his cheek and a busted lip.

"Sachi," Emily said, "we have to get out of here and get help."

"I won't leave him." She stroked his cheek and slipped his head onto her lap. "I won't let them hurt him anymore."

"We have to get help, or we won't be able to help any of them. We can't carry Tyler out and the women are too drugged to help themselves."

"Then go," Sachi said. "Get help. I must stay."

Emily would get nowhere with the woman and she couldn't blame her for insisting on staying with the man she loved. But if someone didn't get off the ship and go for help, none of them would be freed.

Emily squared her shoulders. "I'll be back with help," she promised.

She turned and ran down the narrow hallway to the nearest door that might lead to an upper deck and a way off the ship.

The passageways were a maze of twists and turns. Finally she found stairs leading upward. She paused at the bottom, listening for sounds of voices or movement above. When she was fairly certain the deck above was clear, she hurried up the stairs. She swallowed a groan as another hallway greeted her. She ran to the end and through an open door. More steps led upward and she could hear the sounds of motors humming and the clanking of metal on metal.

Emily eased up the stairs until she could see the upper deck and stacks of shipping containers lined in neat rows, filling the top deck of the ship, bathed in stadium lights. A crane lowered another metal box onto a stack. Men shouted and waved to the man operating the crane.

The boom turned back to the shore and stopped, the engine shutting down.

More men hurried around the deck, securing lines, apparently preparing the ship to leave. Some of the stevedores crossed the gangway to the shore, waving to the men remaining on the ship.

Emily slipped out onto the deck, moving among the shadows. She worked her way to the side of the ship and looked over the edge.

The ship rose forty feet out of the water. The dock was at least ten feet away and twenty feet below where she stood. If she made a flying leap, she could miss the dock and fall the forty feet into the water. If she landed wrong in the water, it could be like hitting concrete. She could die before she got help for the others in the hold below.

No, she had to use the gangway if she wanted to get off in one piece. She'd be exposed and possibly caught, but she had to do something or they would all be lost.

Emily waited until the majority of the deckhands were looking the other way and then made her run for it. She made it to the gangway and put one foot onto the metal grate when hands reached out and grabbed her.

"I cannot have my guest leaving so very soon," a man said, his tone deep and threatening.

Emily glanced over her shoulder into the black eyes of Viktor Sokolov, the ambassador's rogue assistant, and he was speaking English.

Chapter Seventeen

"She's on board that one." Mack pointed to the container ship secured at the dock.

Mustang pushed past Mack but was stopped in his tracks when Declan reached out to capture his arm. "We can't just go storming aboard. We need a plan."

"Hell, we need to take a page from our enemy's book and create a diversion," Mack said.

Clenching his fists, Mustang turned to their slack man, Jack Snow. "What have we got?"

Snow grinned and dropped a duffel bag at the team's feet. "I'm glad you asked. You'd be surprised at the variety of munitions Charlie's husband stockpiled in the basement beneath the garage. He has enough weapons to man a small army and enough ammunition to last long enough to survive a zombie apocalypse."

"I'm not interested in a zombie apocalypse. I want to get Emily the hell off that ship in one piece."

"You know, we're not in Afghanistan anymore. Perhaps we should call the police and let them handle this," Cole suggested.

The other five members of the team stared at him as if he'd lost his mind.

"If we involve the police, they might decide to kill Emily and Sachi and cut their losses." Mustang tipped his head toward the ship.

"Or there will be a big political standoff with the Russian government and the Russian bad guys might commit murder and suicide to keep from being sent to Siberia," Mack said.

Mustang shook his head. "We can't risk it. We have to go in, neutralize the threat and free the hostages. It's what we do. What we're good at." He waved his hand. "Show me what you've got."

Snow pulled out four M4A1 rifles, two submachine guns and magazines filled with bullets for both, half a dozen smoke grenades, a small brick of C4 explosive and the detonators to go with it. He'd also brought six K-Bar knives and their sheaths, and body armor.

"Damn, Snow." Cole laughed. "You don't happen to have a rocket launcher tucked into that, do you?"

"No, but I'm sure Charlie can get you hooked up with one," Snow said with a straight face. "Just say the word."

Declan handed the C4 to Mack. "Make a noise, not enough to sink the ship, but enough to be heard and scare the crew ashore."

Mack took the C4. "How am I supposed to get on board the ship to do that?"

Snow hefted two of the smoke grenades. "I played outfield on my baseball team in high school. Had the best and most accurate distance throwing arm on the team."

"Can you get those smoke grenades on board that ship from the dock?" Declan asked.

"Just point. I'll deliver."

"We need one at the far end of the ship. If that doesn't make them think they have a ship-board fire, we can toss the other in for good measure," Declan said.

"You've got it."

"Mustang, you're point man," Declan said. "As soon as the crew bails, you're first man in. We'll be right behind you."

Mack showed Mustang the tracking device. "If this is accurate through the metal hull, Emily is somewhere near the bridge."

"I'll cover Mustang's six," Declan said. "Mack, you and Cole set the charges, Gus and Snow cover the gangway and keep anyone from coming back on board once they've disembarked. Our goal is to get in there, retrieve Emily and Sachi, and get the hell out before we're caught in an international incident."

Mack snorted. "What would it hurt? We've already got dishonorable discharges on our records," he said, referring to their refusal to handle a kill that would have involved too much collateral damage during their military days.

Declan claimed a submachine gun and the rounds that went with it. "No matter what the records show, we're honorable men. As long as we keep that in mind, that's all that counts."

"And if the body count mounts?" Gus asked as he buckled his protective vest in place.

"We'll cross that bridge when we get to it. *If* we get to it," Declan said, slipping his body armor over his shoulder.

Once the rest of the men had their bullet-proof vests on, Declan asked, "Ready?"

As one, the team replied. "Ready."

Anxious to get started, Mustang checked his handgun in the holster on his hip, grabbed one of the rifles and slipped several magazines into the pouches on his body armor and moved forward through the maze of containers, keeping to the shadows. He wouldn't get ahead of the plan. He'd been with these men long enough to know the value of teamwork and having someone to cover him when he took point.

The bright lights of the shipyard cast deep

shadows alongside the large, metal shipping containers, giving Mustang the concealment he needed to get close to the ship.

When he was as near as he could get without being seen, he waited for the signal to board… that signal being the launch of the smoke grenades.

He didn't have long to wait. From his position he could see the arch of the grenade as it flew through the air and landed on the ship's bow, rolling among the stacks of containers. A puff of smoke rose on impact and spread all across that end of the ship.

Shouts echoed in the night and men ran for fire extinguishers. When they couldn't locate the source of the smoke, some made the decision to abandon ship. A dozen men crossed the gangplank.

In the ensuing smoke and confusion, Mustang tucked his rifle against his leg, walked past the men leaving, and boarded the ship, keeping his head down so that anyone he passed wouldn't immediately realize he was a stranger.

Once on board, he waited for Declan to catch up, keeping a close watch for anyone who might be a danger to his teammate.

Declan walked on board, the submachine gun hidden beneath his jacket.

With the tracking device in hand, Mustang headed for the tallest part of the ship and the wheelhouse where the captain commanded the operation of the ship.

Several times before he reached the pilot castle, Mustang had to duck back against the containers to avoid being seen by armed men running around in the smoke.

With Declan covering him, Mustang entered the pilot castle and climbed the steps up to the deck where the bridge was located. At the top, he surprised two guards standing watch at a door Mustang assumed led to the bridge.

Before the men could aim their weapons, Mustang swung the butt of his rifle, hitting the first one in the nose at the same time as he threw a side kick into the other guard's gut. He had them both subdued by the time Declan joined him on the deck.

Wordlessly, Mustang eased open the door to the bridge, holding his rifle at the ready.

Not ten feet from where he was, Mustang spotted Emily standing at the center of the window that stretched from one end of the room to the other.

She was turned to face the door from which Mustang viewed her.

She shook her head imperceptibly and shot a glance to her right.

Mustang's gaze followed Emily's to a man with thick gray hair and piercing black eyes, holding a gun pointed at her chest.

"Come in," the man said. "Please, join my other guest."

Emily shook her head more noticeably. "Don't," she said. "He's got a gun."

"Oh, but I insist. And if you do not come in, I will shoot the interpreter."

Mustang entered, aiming his rifle at the man's chest. "You must be Viktor Sokolov," he guessed.

Sokolov dipped his head in acknowledgment. "I am. And you must be our little interpreter's bodyguard who has made it difficult for us to dispose of her."

Mustang's chest tightened. "Why would you want to kill her? What did she ever do to you?"

Viktor's eyes narrowed. "It is not what she did, but what she witnessed."

"The journalist you detained in the embassy?" Mustang asked. "Where is he now? Or have you disposed of him, as well?"

"All in due time," Viktor said. "It is much easier to dispose of a body at sea than on land."

"And is that what you have planned for Miss Chastain?" Mustang hoped that by keeping the man talking, he'd buy some time to come up with a plan to save Emily.

"Now that she is here, it seems a waste to do away with her, especially when we can get a sizeable sum for a woman with her particular shade of blond hair. And blue eyes are prized."

Mustang muttered a curse beneath his breath. The bastard was trafficking women to foreign markets, and he planned on selling Emily to the highest bidder. Death was too kind for Viktor.

"Don't worry about me," Emily said. "Just shoot the bastard. There are more people at stake here."

Mustang aimed his gun at the man's chest, beyond tempted to pull the trigger.

Viktor snorted. "Shoot me, and you are all dead."

"What do you mean?" Emily asked.

"There are explosives aboard this ship, rigged with a timer. I set it for fifteen minutes…five minutes ago. I am the only one who knows where the explosives are and the only one with the code to disarm the detonator."

Mustang shot a glance at this watch. Ten minutes wasn't enough time to do anything, much less search an entire ship for explosives and disarm said explosives. "You're bluffing."

Viktor's lips curled. "Are you certain? Only time will tell. Now, enough talk. You will clear this ship of all of your personnel in five minutes."

"This ship is worth more than the cargo it carries. Put down your weapon and give up now and you might not get the death penalty."

Viktor shook his head. "Nine minutes and counting. You are meddling in something much bigger than the cost of just one ship. An organization that extends beyond my little portion of the operation. There are people all over the world who will not be happy if they are exposed. People in your own country. In your own government." He chuckled. "I will not give up."

"Let Miss Chastain go and I'll see to it that you are free to go," Mustang lied. "And I'm sure the Russian ambassador would pay dearly to get his daughter back."

The ambassador's assistant shook his head. "You are a fool. Eight minutes."

While Viktor's attention was focused on Mustang, Emily inched toward her captor.

Mustang wanted to tell her to stand fast, to keep from becoming Viktor's next victim. But to say anything would divert Viktor's attention back to her.

He didn't have to ponder that dilemma. In a

flash, Emily dove for the gun in Viktor's hand and shoved it toward the floor.

The sound of a gunshot blasted through the air.

Mustang aimed at Viktor, but couldn't pull the trigger for fear of hitting Emily.

She had hold of the man's wrist, struggling to keep it pointed at the floor, but the man was strong. Slowly he overpowered her, inching the gun toward her chest.

Mustang had to do something. He couldn't stand by and let Viktor kill the woman who'd come to mean more to him than he'd ever imagined a woman could in such a short time. He aimed his gun and pulled the trigger, praying Emily didn't shift at the last moment.

Two gunshots echoed across the bridge.

Viktor slumped over, his body landing on top of Emily's, crushing her beneath him.

Mustang's breath lodged in his throat until Emily's hand moved. "Help," she said, her voice strained and breathy.

Mustang ran to her, shoved Viktor over and bent to Emily. Blood covered her shirt.

"I couldn't get in to help in case Viktor got spooked and pulled the trigger prematurely," Declan said, entering the room behind Mustang. "I texted Mack and told him to hold off on the explosives. We don't know if a small explosion will trigger whatever Viktor has set. Is Emily okay?"

"I don't know." Mustang stared into Emily's gaze. "Were you hit?"

Emily stared at the blood, her eyes widening. She patted her chest and abdomen and let out a sigh. "It's not mine. I'm okay." She struggled to stand. "How many minutes do we have left?" she demanded.

Mustang looked at his watch. "Five."

"We have to help the others." Emily ran for the door.

"Wait!" Mustang caught her arm, bringing her to a stop. "We don't know if there are more guards."

"I don't care. There are nearly thirty drugged women that I know of belowdecks, as well as Sachi and Tyler Blunt. We can't take the risk Viktor was bluffing. We have to get them out now. And some can't get out on their own." She shook free of his grasp and ran, heading down stairs into the bowels of the ship.

Mustang raced after her, leaping down the stairs two at a time.

"I'm right behind you," Declan called out. "I'll let the others know we'll need help below."

A couple decks below the bridge, Emily came to a halt. Women filled the hallway, some staggering, others leaning on those who could help.

Emily entered one of the doors, helped a woman to her feet and half carried, half dragged her out into the hallway. "This way," Emily said and led the way up the stairs.

Mustang's heart sank when he saw how many women there were in the small, dark room. He shot a glance at his watch. Four minutes. They could only do the best they could. He lifted a limp form off the floor and tossed it over his shoulder. "Follow me," he said and looped an arm around a woman staggering in the hallway. He powered up the stairs, out onto the deck, refusing to let the struggling woman slow him down. Once he had them off the ship, he laid the limp woman on the ground. "Take care of her," he said to the others.

Emily had already returned to the ship.

Three minutes.

Mustang passed Mack, Cole and Gus on their way out, helping two women each. Some of the ladies made it out on their own. When he returned to the lower deck, he found Sachi in the hallway. "Help me, please," she said. "It's Tyler. He's hurt." She led him into a different room where Tyler Blunt attempted to push to his feet.

"Get her out of here," Tyler said as he leaned heavily against the wall.

"Tyler," Sachi said, "I'm not leaving without you." She hooked his arm over her shoulder.

Mustang looped the man's other arm over his shoulder. Between him and Sachi, they got him up the stairs and out onto the deck.

"I can make it from here," Tyler insisted. "Go. Help the others."

With only two minutes remaining, Mustang returned to the lower deck, determined to find Emily and get her out before the ship exploded.

He passed Snow with a woman folded over his shoulder.

"Emily. Have you seen her?"

Snow jerked his head toward the rear. "She was checking the rest of the rooms on this corridor to make sure we didn't leave anyone behind."

"Hurry, get her out of here," Mustang said, nodding at the woman on Snow's shoulder. "We only have seconds to spare."

"Same to you, man." Snow ran down the corridor and up the stairs.

Emily emerged from a room at the end of the hallway. "The rooms are all empty except one." She stood in front of one, her hand on the locking lever.

Deep voices sounded from inside, yelling in Russian.

Emily glanced at Mustang. "They were the men who kidnapped us and brought us to Viktor."

"Go," Mustang said. "Get out of here. We don't have any time left."

"What about them?" she asked, tilting her head at the door. "We can't leave them to die."

"I'll let them out. But I don't want you anywhere near." He turned her toward the stairs. "The longer you take to leave, the more chance of them and me dying in the explosion. If you care at all for me, you'll go."

She shook her head, leaned up on her toes and kissed him full on the lips. "I care," she said. "A lot. I'm going, but I don't want to leave you here." She turned and ran for the stairs.

Mustang grabbed the lock and shoved it to the side. Heaving a sigh, he spun the wheel handle.

As soon as it hit a full stop, the door erupted outward.

Mustang was ready. He jumped back and came out fighting. "Get out of here," he yelled even as he blocked a right jab. "The ship is about to explode," he warned.

The two men weren't listening or couldn't speak English. Either way, Mustang wouldn't make it out in less than a minute. Not if he had to fight his way through the two men. But he wouldn't go down without trying.

He threw a side kick, hitting the bigger guy in the gut. Then he spun and slugged the other man in the chin. Before he could cock his arm to swing again, he was caught from behind by the big guy and his arms were yanked behind him.

The man he'd just clocked in the chin balled his fists and snarled.

A shout in Russian from the other end of the corridor made all three men turn.

Emily stood like an avenging angel with her fists on her hips and her blue eyes blazing. She shouted again in Russian. The two men stared at her, eyes narrowing.

She spoke again, this time in a more urgent tone, and pointed upward.

The big guy said something to the one with his arms cocked, ready to throw a punch.

The man jabbed hard to Mustang's middle, and then he turned and started toward Emily.

Pain made Mustang double over.

The big guy let go and shoved him forward. Then he ran and followed his partner.

Mustang swept out his foot, caught the big man's ankle with his own and sent him sprawling across the narrow hallway and slamming into his partner.

Mustang stepped on top of both men on his way to Emily. He grabbed her hand and ran with her up the steps to the deck above.

They had just made it onto the gangway when the first explosion shook the ship.

The gangway rattled violently.

Mustang grabbed Emily around the waist and leaped for the dock. Behind him the gangway shuddered and buckled, falling into the water.

"Run!" Mustang shouted. Holding Emily's hand, he rushed with her, aiming for the other side of a huge stack of shipping containers.

As he reached the stack, another explosion rumbled inside the ship and then fire and debris shot out of the middle of the stacks of containers, flinging metal shrapnel in every direction.

Mustang pushed Emily behind the containers and dove in after her.

All the women and the rest of his team had taken cover behind the stacks of giant metal boxes.

Mustang didn't relax until he could see every one of Declan's Defenders. Sachi and Tyler were there, too.

He lay on the ground beside Emily, laughter bubbling up his throat.

Emily leaned up on one elbow and frowned down at him. "What's so funny?"

He pulled Emily into his arms and kissed her hard. "Nothing. I'm just so thankful you made it out alive. And, wow, I wish you could have seen yourself shouting at the Russians." A chuckle escaped his chest, relieving the past two days of stress he'd been under. "You were amazing." He kissed her again. "Thank you for saving me."

"Thank you for shooting Viktor and not me," she said and chuckled. "You had me worried for a moment there."

"I had me worried." He smoothed a hand through her hair. "I've never met a woman as courageous as you."

"And I've never met a man who is as determined as you are to keep me safe." She cupped his chin in her palm and brushed her lips across his in a butterfly-soft kiss. "Where do we go from here, now that we know who was behind the attacks on me, Jay and Tyler? I won't need a bodyguard anymore."

"Sweetheart, you're not getting rid of me that easily. Now that I've found you, I won't let you go. I can't. I think I'm falling in love with you."

Epilogue

Emily sat across the dining table from Charlie Halverson. Mustang occupied the seat to her right and Grace the one to her left. "I guess tonight is my last night here at the Halverson estate. Thank you for putting me up for one more night."

"It didn't make any sense for you to go back to your apartment so late when your clothes and toiletries were here," Charlie said. "Besides, I love the company." She smiled around the table at the six men of Declan's Defenders. "While you all were helping the first responders sort through the women and Tyler Blunt, Jonah and I were digging into Viktor Sokolov's personal emails and data files. Since we were able to focus on him, and not all of the embassy staff, we had more success uncovering what he was up to.

"His emails contained information about meeting locations where he collected women.

He used a kind of code to describe each to potential buyers. His buyers are all over the world, including contacts in Saudi Arabia, England, Germany, Bangladesh, Japan and Turkey to name only a few." She frowned and pushed a sheet of paper into the center of the table.

On the paper was a design Emily had seen before. "That's a Celtic knot, a symbol of interconnectedness of all life." She looked from it to Charlie. "What does it have to do with Sokolov and him selling women into the sex trade?"

Mustang tapped the symbol with his finger. "We seem to keep running across it. First Grace found mention of it at Quest Aerospace when she was searching through Riley Lansing's boss's files. He was involved in selling secret blueprints to the Russians."

"And then we saw it again in the ring Riley's sleeper-agent handler had given to her before she died," Mack said, looping his arm over the back of Riley Lansing's chair.

"And Charlie's husband had a similar ring with the same Russian inscription on the inside."

Declan pulled out his smart phone and showed Emily the picture of the inscription.

Emily nodded. "It reads the equivalent of *Always and Forever*." She slipped her hand into

Mustang's. "I'm not sure of the significance of the inscription."

Jack Snow ventured a guess. "It could mean that once the person was a part of the Trinity organization, he or she could never escape."

"Whatever it means, it's making me nervous. It seems we're running into it for a reason," Charlie said. "I just wish we knew what that reason was."

Emily sighed. "I'd like to get some fresh air before I call it a night. It's been a long day."

"You should be able to enjoy the rose garden," Charlie said, "now that no one is waiting to attack you." She gave Emily a reassuring smile.

Mustang jumped up from his seat as Emily stood. "I'll go with her, just to make sure she's safe."

Emily's pulse kicked up a notch and her breathing became more labored at the thought of being alone in the dark with Mustang.

They entered the study and exited the house through the French doors.

Immediately, Emily's senses were bombarded with the aroma of blooming roses.

Mustang captured her hand in his and held on as they walked deeper into the rose garden.

When she reached the fountain with the stone benches surrounding it, she paused.

"This place is magical. I can see why Charlie loves living here."

Mustang turned her to him. "To me, it's the people who make the place. And right now, you're making it magical just by being you."

"A marine and a poet?" She laid her hands on his chest and could feel his heart beating beneath her fingertips. "Does that mean I'll see you again?"

"I hope so," he said and brushed a strand of her hair away from her cheek. "It's up to you. Would you like to go out with me?"

"Yes," she said, her voice breathy, as if she'd been running hard, when in actuality she'd been holding her breath, praying he'd ask. "I'd love to go out with you."

"Hmm. There's that L-word." Mustang kissed the tip of her nose. "Are you one of those women who believes in love at first sight?"

She shrugged. "How am I supposed to answer that? If I say yes, I might scare you away. If I say no, you might think I'm not a romantic, when I am, very much so."

He touched a finger to her lips. "To set the record straight, I never thought I believed in love at first sight until I met you."

Emily laughed. "Your first sight of me was one where I had twigs in my hair and a gun pointed at my head. How could you love that?"

"You were so brave." He kissed her forehead and then each of her eyelids.

Emily's knees threatened to buckle under his tenderness.

"So, do you?" he asked.

She couldn't seem to think when he held her and kissed her like that. "Do I what?"

He kissed her long and hard, pushing his tongue past her teeth to caress hers in a sensuous glide.

When he brought his head up, his gaze met hers reflecting in the moonlight the full force of the emotion Emily felt for him.

"Do you believe in love at first sight?" he said as his mouth skimmed across hers so lightly it left her wanting more.

"Yes," she said and wrapped her arms around his neck to bring his lips back to hers.

* * * * *

Get 4 FREE REWARDS!

We'll send you 2 FREE Books plus 2 FREE Mystery Gifts.

Harlequin Presents® books feature a sensational and sophisticated world of international romance where sinfully tempting heroes ignite passion.

FREE
Value Over
$20

YES! Please send me 2 FREE Harlequin Presents® novels and my 2 FREE gifts (gifts are worth about $10 retail). After receiving them, if I don't wish to receive any more books, I can return the shipping statement marked "cancel." If I don't cancel, I will receive 6 brand-new novels every month and be billed just $4.55 each for the regular-print edition or $5.80 each for the larger-print edition in the U.S., or $5.49 each for the regular-print edition or $5.99 each for the larger-print edition in Canada. That's a savings of at least 11% off the cover price! It's quite a bargain! Shipping and handling is just 50¢ per book in the U.S. and $1.25 per book in Canada.* I understand that accepting the 2 free books and gifts places me under no obligation to buy anything. I can always return a shipment and cancel at any time. The free books and gifts are mine to keep no matter what I decide.

Choose one: ☐ **Harlequin Presents®**
Regular-Print
(106/306 HDN GNWY)

☐ **Harlequin Presents®**
Larger-Print
(176/376 HDN GNWY)

Name (please print)

Address   Apt. #

City   State/Province   Zip/Postal Code

> Mail to the **Reader Service:**
> **IN U.S.A.:** P.O. Box 1341, Buffalo, NY 14240-8531
> **IN CANADA:** P.O. Box 603, Fort Erie, Ontario L2A 5X3

Want to try 2 free books from another series? Call 1-800-873-8635 or visit www.ReaderService.com.

---

*Terms and prices subject to change without notice. Prices do not include sales taxes, which will be charged (if applicable) based on your state or country of residence. Canadian residents will be charged applicable taxes. Offer not valid in Quebec. This offer is limited to one order per household. Books received may not be as shown. Not valid for current subscribers to Harlequin Presents books. All orders subject to approval. Credit or debit balances in a customer's account(s) may be offset by any other outstanding balance owed by or to the customer. Please allow 4 to 6 weeks for delivery. Offer available while quantities last.

Your Privacy—The Reader Service is committed to protecting your privacy. Our Privacy Policy is available online at www.ReaderService.com or upon request from the Reader Service. We make a portion of our mailing list available to reputable third parties that offer products we believe may interest you. If you prefer that we not exchange your name with third parties, or if you wish to clarify or modify your communication preferences, please visit us at www.ReaderService.com/consumerschoice or write to us at Reader Service Preference Service, P.O. Box 9062, Buffalo, NY 14240-9062. Include your complete name and address.

HP19R3

Get 4 FREE REWARDS!

We'll send you 2 FREE Books plus 2 FREE Mystery Gifts.

FREE Value Over **$20**

Both the **Romance** and **Suspense** collections feature compelling novels written by many of today's best-selling authors.

YES! Please send me 2 FREE novels from the Essential Romance or Essential Suspense Collection and my 2 FREE gifts (gifts are worth about $10 retail). After receiving them, if I don't wish to receive any more books, I can return the shipping statement marked "cancel." If I don't cancel, I will receive 4 brand-new novels every month and be billed just $6.99 each in the U.S. or $7.24 each in Canada. That's a savings of at least 13% off the cover price. It's quite a bargain! Shipping and handling is just 50¢ per book in the U.S. and $1.25 per book in Canada.* I understand that accepting the 2 free books and gifts places me under no obligation to buy anything. I can always return a shipment and cancel at any time. The free books and gifts are mine to keep no matter what I decide.

Choose one: ☐ **Essential Romance** ☐ **Essential Suspense**
(194/394 MDN GNNP)   (191/391 MDN GNNP)

Name (please print)

Address   Apt. #

City   State/Province   Zip/Postal Code

Mail to the **Reader Service:**
IN U.S.A.: P.O. Box 1341, Buffalo, NY 14240-8531
IN CANADA: P.O. Box 603, Fort Erie, Ontario L2A 5X3

Want to try 2 free books from another series! Call 1-800-873-8635 or visit www.ReaderService.com.